The idea was too outrageous to entertain, let alone voice, and yet she heard herself say, "You could marry me."

"Marry you?" Stephen came forward until he stood just in front of her. "Why would you want to marry me?" His lips thinned into a smile. "Let me guess: this would be your way of paying back your ex-fiancé. A little bit of revenge from the woman scorned."

She nodded. "Yes. As much as I want the good guy to win, I'd also like to see the bad guy lose."

"Are you sure I'm the good guy, Catherine?" His gaze locked with hers in seeming challenge.

For the first time in her life Catherine handed herself over to fate. This was the right thing to do. She could feel it.

"I want you to be," she whispered.

Jackie Braun began making up stories almost as soon as she learned how to write them down. She never wavered from her goal of becoming a professional writer, but a steady diet of macaroni cheese packet meals during college convinced her of the need for a reliable income. She earned her bachelor's degree in journalism from Central Michigan University in 1987, and continues to work as an editorial writer for a daily newspaper. Fiction remains her first love. She lives with her husband and son in Michigan.

Recent titles by the same author:

HER STAND-IN GROOM

BY

JACKIE BRAUN

MILLS & BOON®

To Mom and Dad:
thanks for passing on your love of reading.

All the characters in this book have no existence outside the imagination of the author, and have no relation whatsoever to anyone bearing the same name or names. They are not even distantly inspired by any individual known or unknown to the author, and all the incidents are pure invention.

*First published in Great Britain 2004
Harlequin Mills & Boon Limited,
Eton House, 18-24 Paradise Road, Richmond, Surrey TW9 1SR*

© Jackie Braun Fridline 2004

ISBN 0-263-83830-7

*Set in Times Roman 10½ on 12½ pt.
02-0604-40138*

*Printed and bound in Spain
by Litografía Rosés, S.A., Barcelona*

CHAPTER ONE

THWACK!

Catherine Canton had made a career of opposing domestic violence, but that didn't keep her from using a bouquet of white roses to smack her prospective groom upside his philandering blond head.

Cursing amid a snowstorm of fragrant petals, Derek Danbury stopped his intimate exploration of the wedding planner's lacy black bra.

"What the—" he began, before turning around completely. Once he had, his expression shifted from irritated to uh-oh.

In an instant he was slicking on the charm, as well as the boyish smile Catherine had once found so irresistible. How could she have been so naïve?

All but shoving the other woman aside, he said, "Sweetheart, I can explain this."

If she hadn't wanted to cry Catherine might have laughed at that absurd proposition. And if the situation hadn't been so wretchedly pathetic she might even have let him try, for the sheer entertainment value such an exercise would provide. Derek was a master at coming up with perfectly innocent reasons for doing the outrageous. She'd often found his justifications amusing, if exasperating. But this wasn't the same as showing up late for dinner with her parents or failing to meet her at some charity function.

No, he'd been helping another woman out of her clothes in the choir loft of a church. The same church where, in less than fifteen minutes, he was supposed to swear before God and their guests to forsake all others.

Catherine had never been blind to his flirtatious nature, but she had foolishly believed that flirtation was all he'd ever engaged in. Oh, there had been tabloid speculation to the contrary, but, as her mother had preached on more than one occasion, those rancid scandal sheets' attempts to sell more papers were hardly a valid enough reason for Catherine to question her engagement to one of the country's most eligible bachelors. This was especially the case, her mother had insisted, since she and Catherine's father had already plunked down so much of their dwindling fortune to give their daughter a memorable society wedding.

And so Catherine, ever the dutiful daughter, had brushed aside her nagging concerns as silly prewedding jitters. She didn't doubt for a minute her mother would be ruing the day she'd insisted on hiring a professional wedding planner.

"I don't need an explanation," Catherine said, as the wedding planner buttoned her blouse and wisely slinked away.

"It's really not what it looked like," Derek replied.

She might have been naïve to believe a notorious

playboy like Derek, heir to the venerable Danbury Department Store chain, was ready to settle down, but with the evidence of his infidelity now made so obvious she would not be thought stupid as well.

Holding up a hand, she said, "Please, don't insult my intelligence."

"Come on, Cath. You have to listen to me."

"Listen to you? What can you say to make this somehow less sordid than it actually is? I won't tolerate lies."

"I love you. That's not a lie." He reached out, caressed her arms through the white silk of her gown. Mere minutes ago she would have believed him. But how could he love her—truly love her—and do this?

She pulled away, her breath hitching. "Don't."

"I'm sorry," he repeated. "I made a mistake."

"Would you still think so if you hadn't gotten caught?" Her voice hiked up an octave, pushed there by pain and disbelief. "My God, Derek, you're in a church. It's our wedding day. And you were…" She shook her head, the image still revoltingly fresh.

"Let's keep our voices down, sweetheart," he urged, casting a nervous glance toward the railing, no doubt thinking about the multitude of guests already assembled below. "In fact, let's discuss this later."

"Later? When later? After we're married?" She crossed her arms and tapped the battered bouquet against one hip, her emotions swinging wildly from hurt to anger again. "I don't think so."

Alarm widened his eyes. "You're overreacting, Cath. Don't blow this out of proportion."

"Oh, that's rich. You almost had sex in the church with our wedding planner minutes before the ceremony. I don't see how I could blow this out of proportion. As offenses go, Derek, what you did is gargantuan already."

"You know, technically I didn't do anything."

Catherine closed her eyes and counted to ten, trying to summon up some of the control for which she was legendary. Ice Princess, some called her, but she was fuming now, a volcano ready to blow. She preferred that. Hurt and embarrassment could come later, and settle over her like suffocating ash. She dropped her hands to her sides. Her fingers fisted around the bouquet handle as if were a Louisville Slugger, and she was seriously thinking about taking another swing at him when someone said, "Excuse me, please."

Derek's cousin Stephen stood not five feet behind them in the choir loft. Despite similar heights and builds, and the fact their birthdays fell just one day apart, she couldn't imagine two men more different in either appearance or disposition. Derek was fair and always joking. Stephen was dark and brooding.

He stepped forward, his voice barely above a whisper. "Derek, your mother asked me to come and mention that the guests can hear this conversation. She suggests you move to a more discreet location."

Whatever he thought of the situation, none of it was reflected in the deep brown of his eyes.

Privacy. Catherine longed for it at this moment—that and something far more comfortable than the beaded pumps that were crushing the toes on each foot into a single digit. But both would have to wait until she'd dealt with the situation at hand. Picking up the heavy train of the designer gown her mother had insisted Catherine had to have, she walked to the railing of the balcony.

"Can I have everyone's attention, please?"

"What are you doing?" Derek whispered, rushing up from behind her. He grabbed her arm none too gently, hauling her around. The act so surprised Catherine that she dropped her bouquet over the rail's edge. Its sterling silver handle struck the tiled aisle below, echoing in the church like a shotgun blast. Guests shifted in their seats to see what was going on, some of them pointing, all of them murmuring.

Catherine gasped. "You're hurting me."

In an instant Stephen was beside them.

"Don't be an idiot, Derek. Let go of her arm." He never raised his voice, in fact he lowered it, and he seemed all the more menacing because of it.

"This isn't your concern, cousin. It's a simple misunderstanding between Catherine and me. We don't require your interference."

"I'll be the one to decide that."

Stephen stepped between them, forcing Derek to break his hold on her arm.

Catherine expelled a breath, still too stunned to believe what had just occurred. Over Stephen's shoulder she stared at Derek, feeling as if she were truly seeing him for the first time. There was no denying he was a beautiful man, with sun-kissed hair and eyes a clear crystal-blue. Had all that physical perfection and his considerable charm somehow blinded her to the ugliness she now saw in his sneering visage?

He glared first at Stephen and then at her, and she could not help but recall the story of Dr. Jekyll and Mr. Hyde, for he seemed so different from the man who had swept her off her feet with words of love and eyes full of adoration.

At last something—manners? breeding?—resurrected itself. His tone hushed, he said, "Have it your way, cousin. I don't really need her anyway."

Need? What an odd way to put it. Before Catherine could puzzle through what he meant by that strange and hurtful statement, he was calling out, "The wedding is off. Catherine and I regret the inconvenience to you all and thank you for your understanding. Please accept our apologies."

The church erupted in full-fledged conversations now. The talk was no longer library-quiet but ballgame-loud, as guests traded speculation about the doomed couple.

Stephen lingered beside Catherine after Derek had stalked away, although he looked uncomfortable to be there.

"Are you all right?" he asked.

She nodded stiffly, even as her heart seemed to shatter into a million jagged pieces.

"I got a note telling me to meet Derek here for a surprise. I thought maybe he'd bought me a gift, something he wanted me to wear down the aisle. Instead, I found him…"

She sucked in a breath, still not quite able to believe what she had witnessed. All that passion, and for a virtual stranger. Had she ever inspired that kind of excitement in her prospective groom? Had she ever felt it in return? Those questions as much as Derek's infidelity forced a sob from her lips. She covered her mouth, muffling another.

"Can I get someone for you? Your mother, perhaps?"

"Dear God!" It came out half-sob, half-hysterical laugh. "Why don't you just dump me over the rail along with my bouquet?"

Her mother was probably hyperventilating at this point. And her poor father had probably fainted dead away after realizing they'd just blown hundreds of thousands of dollars, much of it non-refundable, on a wedding that would never take place. At least he would have all that twelve-year-old Scotch to commiserate with. For a daughter who had spent a lifetime trying to please her difficult parents, she'd certainly made a mess of things.

"I'll take that as a no." A ghost of a smile hovered on his lips.

They were nice lips, a little fuller than most men's, softening the otherwise hard lines of his face. Catherine could only recall having half a dozen conversations with Stephen, all of them about polite, neutral topics. The cousins didn't share the same interests or circle of friends, but whenever she did spend time in his company, or whenever she ran into him while visiting Derek at the Danbury building, she found herself undeniably drawn to Stephen.

She sensed a sadness about him, a loneliness that she always assumed resulted from losing his mother and father as a boy and being raised by his stodgy grandparents. It was in Catherine's nature to soothe, to nurture, to comfort. That was the source of the odd attraction, she'd told herself when she'd first begun to feel it. Now, with her emotions reeling, she wasn't so sure. In fact, she wasn't sure of anything.

He cleared his throat, and she realized she had been staring at him.

Summoning up her manners, Catherine said, "Thank you for what you did just now. I don't know what came over Derek, grabbing my arm that way."

"Did he hurt you?"

Her arm ached, but she resisted the urge to rub it. "No, not really," she lied. "I hope there won't be a strain between the two of you because of this?"

Again that enigmatic smile lurked, although this time she thought he seemed a little resigned. "I'm sure this won't change a thing."

"Well, thank you anyway."

Stephen watched her leave, spilling out the train of white silk as she walked down the stairs. He knew from his aunt's endless chatter that the gown was an original, designed especially for this bride. The small pearl buttons that ran the length of Catherine's slender spine were the real thing, as were the tiny pearls that edged the neckline. He wondered if it disappointed Catherine that no one would see its beauty this day as she glided down the aisle on her father's arm. He knew it would most women of her sort.

Debutante. The word alone left a sour taste in his mouth. Admittedly, his opinion of Catherine was colored by his opinion of his cousin. Any woman who would consent to marry Derek surely had to be as shallow and self-centered as he. Still, Stephen was glad she'd discovered what kind of man her prospective groom really was before making a lifetime commitment. Stephen's regard for her had jumped several notches, watching her dump Derek just before the "I dos" were exchanged. She had literally lost a fortune by doing so, regardless of the prenuptial agreement she had signed.

Downstairs, people were already streaming from the pews, many of them heading straight for her, with pity pinching their mouths into thin smiles. Stephen felt a twinge of it for her as well. No one should be forced to listen graciously to trite and in some cases insincere condolences right after what Catherine had been through. But as he watched her summon up what he thought of as her serene society expression he knew she would handle this with her usual cool grace. That was what debs did, and Catherine Canton did it better than most.

Turning, he saw his aunt heading in his direction, high heels clicking on the tile floor. If not for the Botox injections Marguerite Bledsoe Danbury had had to reduce the wrinkles on her forehead and around her eyes, he knew she would be scowling. But the injections had frozen her face into an eerie mask of youthful blankness. Add to that the signature red hair, which she wore longer than most women her age, and a figure that had been liposuctioned and tucked to trimness, and she appeared a good fifteen years younger than her fifty-nine years.

"A word with you, please," she said when she reached him. Snagging Stephen's sleeve, she led him to a corner, which provided a modicum of privacy.

"Where is Derek?" Despite that bland expression, her eyes burned with fury.

"I haven't seen him since he left the choir loft," Stephen replied. He'd bet his inheritance his cousin was long gone, leaving it to others to clean up his latest mess. His aunt must have reached that conclusion, too.

"There are a dozen reporters and photographers, most of them tabloid, hanging around outside, waiting for a shot of the new Mrs. Danbury. I want Catherine out of here. Now."

Her first concern, as always, was herself. The young woman who would have become her daughter-in-law was now merely a liability to be dealt with.

"I'm sure her parents will take her home."

"See that they do."

It was not a request but a command. Marguerite never asked Stephen for anything. She made demands and expected her demands to be met without question or complaint. Stephen acceded to her wishes, even though he thought Catherine might have had enough of the Danburys for one day. Still, he'd rather she had to face him than his aunt.

He heard Catherine's voice as he approached the bride's room. The emotion he'd detected earlier, when he'd overheard her conversation with Derek, had been carefully edited out. "I'm fine, Mother, really."

"It's too bad about the wedding," her younger sister Felicity said. "You look stunning in that dress."

Stephen rapped his knuckles on the semi-open door. "Excuse me," he said. "May I come in?"

Catherine glanced over at him and he witnessed for a brief instant the strain she otherwise hid so well. She smiled, revealing an odd little dimple just to the left of her chin, a small bit of imperfection that somehow only enhanced the beauty of her classical Grace Kelly features.

"Of course."

He stepped into the room, closing the door.

"Stephen, dear, I was just telling Catherine not to let this little indiscretion ruin things," her mother said. "She and Derek can put this behind them."

In their social sphere, he knew, infidelity was often brushed under the rug. Wives weren't supposed to make waves, at least not publicly, and husbands were supposed to be discreet in their dalliances. Times might have changed, but obviously that was the pabulum still being force-fed to each new batch of old-money debs.

"I hope she doesn't share your opinion," he said, his gaze never leaving Catherine's.

"Well, I do," Felicity said. "I'd marry him, and keep this incident as leverage."

Catherine's sister was eighteen years old, and though he'd only met her on a couple of occasions just before the wedding, she appeared to be as spoiled as she was outspoken.

Catherine sent Stephen a bemused smile, but said nothing as her sister and mother continued to chatter on about the mistake she was making.

"My aunt sent me to tell you there is a limousine outside when you are ready to leave. The tabloid photographers are lining up, and surely more are on the way."

"Oh, dear," her mother said, fanning her face. "This is such an embarrassment."

Catherine looked embarrassed, all right, but Stephen didn't think it had anything to do with Derek at that moment. She reached up, as if to take off her veil.

"I wouldn't take the time to change," Stephen advised, knowing full well that a woman in shorts and a tank top could require half an hour. Who knew how long a woman in full wedding regalia would need to undress?

"He's right, Catherine. Gather up your things. You

can change at the house. Felicity, go find your father.''

"The house?" A pair of finely arched brows shot
up in question. "I'd like to go back to my apartment,
Mother. I hope you don't mind, but I'd like to be
alone.''

"Nonsense. You'll come to the house.''

It was if she hadn't spoken at all, Stephen thought.
Worse, it was as if she were a child, rather than a
grown woman of twenty-eight. He watched as she
turned and began to gather up her belongings, but
then she dumped them back onto the vanity and
marched to the door.

"Where are you going?" Deirdra Canton called.

Catherine's gaze never strayed from Stephen's.
"I'm leaving. Now. I'll call you in the morning.''

Stephen didn't say a word. He simply opened the
door, took Catherine by the arm and led her away.

"Thank you," she said a moment later. "That's
twice you've come to my rescue today.''

He shrugged off her appreciation. "Don't thank me
yet. We still have to outwit the paparazzi.''

He hustled her out the rectory door, but the photographers, as if scenting blood, were already there.
Stephen blocked as much of their view of her as possible, holding her close and hovering around her like
a bodyguard.

"Get in the limo," he said, all but pushing her
inside the door he'd already opened. Behind them
flashes popped and people shouted out their names.

Inside, even with the tinted windows, she huddled low on the seat opposite his, looking shell-shocked and shaken.

"I never dreamed this would be how I left the church on my wedding day. I feel like some hideous car crash, gawked at and then gossiped over."

"Hideous" was hardly the word that came to his mind as he looked at her lovely oval face, with its finely arched eyebrows and dark-fringed eyes the color of sapphires. A man could drown in those eyes. He glanced away. Perhaps Derek had, and that was why he'd considered trading in bachelorhood for permanent couple status when monogamy had never been his strong suit.

"Don't worry. It won't last forever. Next week some major star will go into rehab and that pack of vultures will be waiting outside the Betty Ford."

She let out a startled laugh. "Is that supposed to be the bright side?"

"Only if you're a desperate optimist. Where do you want to go? I don't suggest returning to your apartment for a while."

She shrugged. "I don't know. I'm open to ideas."

To the chauffeur he said, "Drive around for a while, but start heading toward the Belmont Yacht Club."

"The yacht club?"

"Trust me."

"Why not? What else have I got to do this eve-

ning?'' she said, her tone dry, her eyes suddenly starting to mist.

He fished a white handkerchief from one of his
pockets and handed it to her. ''Here.''

''I'm not crying,'' she said, sounding slightly offended. But she didn't look at him, and even in profile
he could see a tear slip down her pale cheek.

An hour later they arrived at the Belmont Yacht Club,
a small and exclusive marina just north of the city.
Catherine had been to the club a number of times with
Derek, who docked his fifty-four-foot cabin cruiser
there, and her own family retained a membership,
even though their yacht had been sold when the stock
market plummeted, taking a good portion of their
heavily invested fortune with it. But she hadn't realized Stephen also boated. He corrected her immediately when she made the observation aloud.

''I sail.''

That surprised her even more. Of course, sailing
would suit someone as quiet and self-contained as
Stephen, but his parents, as well as Derek's father,
had died in a sailing accident on this very lake when
the boys were barely out of diapers.

He helped her from the limo, and then spoke to the
driver as she tried to smooth out the crumpled silk of
her dress.

''Meet us back here around one.'' Handing the man
a sizable tip, he added, ''And if anyone asks, you
never saw us.''

He grabbed the champagne that had been chilling in an ice bucket in the back of the limo and started for the waterfront, leaving her with little choice but to follow him. Along the way they passed a couple of bikini-clad young women, coming in from a lazy day spent out on the lake.

"Congratulations!" one called. To her companion she murmured, "I wonder which boat they're going to be rocking?"

And Catherine realized how it must look: Stephen in a tuxedo; she wearing her wedding finery. It was as if they were a couple, setting out for a romantic sunset cruise on Lake Michigan to toast their nuptials and kick off their honeymoon in style.

He must have realized it, too. His gaze swerved to hers, held for a lingering moment, but he said nothing.

Several slips down from Derek's luxurious cruiser, he swung aboard a graceful sailboat. It was much smaller than Derek's yacht, which took a five-man crew to operate. But at thirty-eight feet, it could hardly be considered little.

Standing on the dock, Catherine said, "What do you call her?"

"*La Libertad.*"

The foreign name rolled from his tongue, sounding like poetry, and he stared at her afterward. His gaze seemed defiant, although she couldn't have said why.

"That's Spanish for freedom, right?"

"Freedom." He nodded.

"She's a beauty. Do you take her out often?"

"As often as I can, which isn't as often as I like. And the season seems to get shorter every year."

"Are we going for a sail?"

"That's my plan."

"I'm afraid I don't know a mast from a jib."

"I've got it covered. Don't worry." He motioned for her to step closer. "Here, let me help you board. We wouldn't want you to wind up bobbing around in Lake Michigan in that gown."

He surprised her with a smile as he said it, reaching out for her waist to help her aboard. She rested her hands on his shoulders, transfixed by the rare smile and offering one of her own in return. Neither of them saw the photographer until they heard the unmistakable whirring of a camera's motor.

"Oh, no! Stop!" Catherine cried, bringing up her hands to shield her face.

Stephen's exclamation was far more graphic. And from his murderous expression she thought he might hop back onto the deck and dump the guy in Lake Michigan, camera and all.

"Get below," he called, pushing her in the direction of the cabin.

The man snapped off several more frames before Stephen managed to shove off from the dock. But Catherine had a feeling the first shot, the one of Stephen smiling as his hands spanned her waist, would be the one that graced the cover of whatever publication the guy worked for. She could only imagine what the accompanying copy would say, especially if the camera angle had also caught her smiling back.

Stephen might prefer sailing, but he used the boat's motor to take them out to open waters. Lake Michigan's vastness was the perfect place to hide in plain sight from the paparazzi. They could hear and see any approaching watercraft long before anyone aboard could click their picture.

She came above deck when she was sure they were safely out of range of even a telephoto lens, and settled onto one of the white padded benches near the wheel where Stephen stood. Just for a moment he reminded her of a pirate. He had shed his suit coat and black tie, and opened the collar of his white shirt, exposing more golden-brown skin. His cuffs were rolled to the forearm. The look on his face was one of relaxed satisfaction. Where he had looked debonair in a tuxedo, now he simply looked dangerous.

Arranging the folds of her gown around her on the bench, she thought it a pity that her own clothing was not so easily converted to casual. She had taken off the veil and tried to bustle her gown without much success. But at least she had finally shed those crippling shoes.

They were still using the boat's low-horsepower motor, which made their progress relatively slow. The motor was only intended for days when the wind failed to co-operate. That wasn't a problem on this evening. She had little doubt that if they had hoisted the sails they would have been halfway to Michigan by now. The wind was strong, breaking small white-caps in the water around them. It ruffled Stephen's dark hair, and it was probably wreaking havoc with the intricate style she'd spent the better part of the morning with a hairdresser to achieve.

"Ever sail before?" he asked.

"Once, as a child, in a small boat my uncle owned. I remember watching the sail tilt almost parallel to the water."

"Exciting, isn't it?"

She recalled only terror and an upset stomach. "I thought I was going to die."

"Well, it's not for everyone."

"But it suits you," she said. And it did. He didn't look quite so remote with the wind making his hair dance and excitement lighting up his dark eyes.

"I opened the champagne." He motioned to the small table in front of her. She couldn't imagine what they had to toast, and she said as much, but he merely shrugged. "There are glasses in the galley, first cup-board on the right, if you wouldn't mind getting them."

When she stood to fetch them she stumbled on her dress. Even as her fingers curled around the rail she felt his hands grip her waist, spanning it as he had when he'd helped her board. He turned her slowly and she caught the subtle scent of his aftershave.

"Steady now."

"If only Vera Wang would make a gown suitable for sailing," she quipped, suddenly ill at ease.

"If you want to take it off, I have something a little more comfortable you can wear."

Had the line come from Derek's mouth it would have been accompanied by a wolfish grin. Stephen merely waited patiently for her reply, no ulterior motive seeming to lurk in his steady gaze. Yet none of her discomfort left.

"That's probably a good idea."

He cut the motor and lowered the anchor before following her below deck, where he gave her the grand tour in under a minute. The cabin had two sleeping quarters, a tiny stall of a bathroom, and a main area that functioned as both kitchen and living room.

"It's small, but efficient," he said as if reading her mind. "And, unlike Derek, I don't need an entire crew to take her out."

That distinction would be important to him, she decided.

He opened the door to the bathroom and pulled a white terry-cloth robe from a hook on the wall. Handing it to her, he said, "I don't think my clothes will fit you. But this should do, even though it's bound to be too big, too."

When he started to leave, she cleared her throat. "Stephen. I...need your help."

He turned slowly, and her breath caught. Limned in the light that streamed from above deck, he seemed otherworldly. And she was about to ask him to help her out of her clothes.

"The buttons." She motioned over her shoulder. "I can't undo them by myself." With a rueful laugh that she hoped would lighten the mood, she admitted, "It took the assistance of two of my bridesmaids to get into this thing."

He said nothing, merely nodded. She turned as he approached, glad to present him with her back, since she felt suddenly awkward and shy. Perhaps that was because her groom should have been the one to help her out of the dress. Indeed, the exercise could have been considered foreplay.

Stephen obviously didn't consider it to be any such thing. He worked in silence, and swiftly, considering his hands were large and the pearls small and slippery.

At the base of her spine, however, he paused, lingered. And she thought she understood why.

"It's a birthmark." The words were barely above a whisper. With a self-conscious laugh, she admitted, "And the reason I've never worn a bikini in my life."

She could have sworn she felt a fingertip gently trace the large heart-shaped freckle that marred her lower back. But then he was handing her the robe.

"Come up when you're ready."

He stopped to retrieve two wineglasses from one of the cupboards in the small galley and then he was gone. Alone, Catherine expelled a breath and tried to find a rational explanation for her shaking hands and pounding heart.

He was sipping champagne when she came above

deck, wearing his robe. As he had predicted, it was much too large for her. At five-seven, she hardly considered herself petite, but it dwarfed her frame, hanging nearly to her ankles. Beneath its hem, her bare feet peeked out.

"I poured you a glass." He motioned to a seat across from his. On the small table between them sat the champagne bottle and an amber-filled flute. He raised his own and sipped again. She sat as well, pulling the robe tightly around her knees, and did the same.

"This can't be how you intended to spend your evening."

He shrugged. "The same could be said for you."

"No." She smiled sadly. "I thought I'd be Mrs. Derek Danbury by this time, listening to the musicians my mother hired slaughter 'We've Only Just Begun.' I can only imagine how upset she and my father are right now."

"I'll apologize for my cousin's poor behavior."

She sipped her champagne, enjoying the warmth it spread through her system. "Why should you? It's not your fault."

"No," he agreed. "But he's a fool. You made a beautiful bride, Catherine."

The compliment came as a surprise, as he didn't seem the sort to issue one easily. And so it warmed her, or perhaps that was just the champagne.

"Thank you. It was the dress. Who wouldn't look good wearing Vera Wang?"

"It was more than the dress," she thought he said, but the wind stole his words. Or maybe that was just what her bruised ego needed to hear.

The waves lapped against the boat's hull, rocking them gently. The rhythm and the wine made her sleepy, but she kept up her end of the conversation, even when he steered it to politics, business practices and current events. They were safe topics, and far more interesting than the usual polite small talk she'd encountered from men, who apparently thought because she wore a bra it meant she couldn't read a newspaper.

It was growing dark, and nearly half of the champagne was gone, but she held out her glass when he presented her with the bottle. After he'd filled it halfway, she said, "If we were at the reception you'd offer a toast."

He shook his head. "I wasn't the best man."

For some reason she wanted to dispute his words. In the end she said, "But as a Danbury surely you would have been expected to speak? What would you have said? I'd like to know."

"I would have wished you every happiness," he replied solemnly, dutifully. And she believed him.

"And now? What is there to toast now?"

She'd asked the question before, but this time Stephen had an answer. Holding up his glass, he said, *"La Libertad."*

The word rolled slowly from his tongue, the R a seductive purr that raised gooseflesh on her arms and left her to wonder whether he meant the sailboat that had spirited her away from reality or her near-brush with matrimony.

"La Libertad," she repeated, her accent not nearly as perfected. She swallowed the last of her champagne and settled her head back against the cushions. Closing her eyes, she said, "I like the sound of that."

CHAPTER TWO

FROM the window of his office, high in the Danbury Building, Stephen watched a sailboat slice through the choppy waves on Lake Michigan. He envied those on board, wishing he could be out there as well, harnessing the wind, outrunning old demons. Soon, too soon, August would give way to September, and then summer to autumn. Not long after that the world would become dormant, *La Libertad* would be put into storage, and ice would make Stephen's favorite place inaccessible for the next several months.

Unbidden came the memory of Catherine Canton, and the way she had looked wearing his bathrobe on that sultry July evening when they had hidden from the paparazzi aboard *La Libertad.*

They'd talked for a few hours, before he'd sailed the boat to port and taken her home. In that time they'd finished the bottle of champagne, and he'd glimpsed the woman beneath all the polish and panache. In addition to her dry sense of humor she possessed a quick wit. She was far smarter, far deeper, far more interesting than he had given her credit for being.

Debutante. The label no longer fit quite so neatly. Or perhaps his admittedly biased definition had

changed. Before that night he'd written her off as
beautiful, but shallow. But a shallow woman did not
keep up on current events, or follow politics. Nor was
she merely a fashionable woman, more interested in
weekly manicures and facials than substantive issues.
She knew designers and followed the latest clothing
trends, he was sure, but she also understood branding,
and in a brief conversation aboard a sailboat, relaxed
by sparkling wine, she'd shown more insight into why
Danbury's was losing customers to its competitors
than many of the people in his own marketing department did.

He'd found himself on the verge of calling her
more than once during the past several weeks, to pick
that finely tuned brain. In the end he hadn't needed
to. She'd called him.

Stephen glanced at his watch. Eleven-fifteen. He
would be meeting her in less than an hour for lunch.
The invitation had surprised him and left him in-
trigued. Business, she'd said. *What exactly did she
want?* He shrugged into his suit coat. He would find
out soon enough.

Catherine discreetly flipped open her compact and
checked her appearance again as she waited in the
restaurant for Stephen to arrive. Why she should be
nervous about seeing him, she didn't know. This was
business, after all. And yet she'd chosen a flowered
silk dress rather than a conservatively cut suit. Okay,
so maybe she had a little crush on her fiancé's—ex-

fiancé's—cousin. It would never amount to anything, of course. They were too different. And yet, after spending that time with him aboard *La Libertad,* she couldn't help but wonder if, beneath it all, they might be very alike.

She dismissed that thought immediately as she watched him enter the restaurant. Stephen Danbury didn't walk so much as stalk, like a big black panther taking stock of his surroundings as he followed the hostess through the crowded dining room. Confident, powerful, in full command. He was a force to be reckoned with. His dark gaze panned the room before settling on her, and Catherine sucked in a breath which she held until he reached their table.

"Your waiter will be with you in a moment," the hostess said. "Can I get you anything to drink?"

"Coffee, black."

When they were alone, he said, "Hello, Catherine."

She held out a hand that was swallowed up in his and offered a smile.

"It's good to see you again, Stephen. And thank you for meeting with me. I know your schedule is very busy."

"I always have time for an intriguing offer."

He seemed to hold her hand a moment longer than was necessary, before finally releasing it and settling into the chair opposite hers.

"What is this business you'd like to discuss?"

No idle chit-chat for him. She'd counted on small

talk and pleasantries to carry them through at least the appetizer. By then she'd hoped to have sufficiently screwed up her courage. She pleated the linen napkin in her lap, a show of nerves she was grateful he could not see.

"Well, as you know, I am the executive director of the Safe Haven Women's Shelter. Our facility houses abused women and their children, helping them get back on their feet emotionally and financially once they've left an abusive relationship."

"A noble effort," he replied, but she couldn't tell from his expression if he meant the words or if he was just being polite.

"We can accommodate up to fifty women and their children. That might seem like a lot, but in a city the size of Chicago it's just a drop in the bucket. In fact, we're full at the moment and we have a waiting list."

"I'm familiar with the shelter and its work," he said.

"Oh." Catherine took a sip of water before continuing. "Then perhaps you are aware that the building we call home is old and in need of substantial repair. I've implemented a fund-raising plan that has helped tremendously. We encourage companies to 'adopt' different apartments in the facility and then refurbish them. Sometimes it's as simple as a fresh coat of paint, carpeting and new bedding. Other rooms need furniture, window treatments, plumbing repairs, light fixtures, rewiring, et cetera. It's a write-off for the companies that participate, and I try to make sure their efforts get adequate coverage in the local media.''

"That's a clever plan."

"I can't take credit for it. Other communities are doing it with great success. I heard about it at a conference I attended."

"It's still a good idea. And you were smart enough to recognize that."

She smiled, ridiculously pleased with the compliment. "Thank you."

The waiter arrived with Stephen's coffee and took their lunch orders, giving Catherine time to mentally prepare the rest of her pitch.

"Recently we received a grant that will cover most of the repair costs for the boiler, so now the roof is our number one priority. It began leaking in the spring, and we had some patching done, but the contractor told us the entire thing should be replaced."

"Roofs can be very expensive."

Catherine cleared her throat and took a sip of her ice water. "Yes, very. Especially on an old building whose structural integrity could be compromised if repairs aren't made soon."

"Which brings us to the point of our lunch meeting, I presume?" He smiled, but his eyes remained unreadable.

"We're hoping Danbury's can help us with a monetary donation that will cover part or all of the roof repairs. I'll personally make sure press releases are sent to the *Tribune* and *Sun-Times*, as well as local televisions stations. I've received three estimates from reputable contractors.'' She pulled papers from her slim leather case and handed them to him.

"You've done your homework."

"I try to be prepared."

He glanced up, his gaze steady. "I enjoy a woman who's prepared."

Nothing in his inscrutable expression revealed whether the double entendre was intentional, but Catherine felt her face grow warm.

"May I keep these?"

When she nodded, he folded the papers and tucked them into his breast pocket without another word.

"You don't need to make a decision right now," she said.

"I didn't plan to." He shifted forward in his seat, leaning over the small table. "Can I ask you something personal, Catherine?"

Her pulse hitched. "Yes."

She realized that she had leaned forward as well when she felt his warm breath on her face as he said, "Why didn't you ever ask Derek about this? He was your fiancé, after all. Talk about a trump card."

She leaned back. "I did. Twice."

Stephen's dark eyebrows shot up. "He never mentioned it to me."

"He kept saying he'd get back to me." She gazed at the linen napkin that lay in twisted heap in her lap. "I don't think he took my work seriously."

"Tonto," he muttered.

"If I'm remembering correctly from my high school Spanish class, you just called Derek a fool."

His use of the word surprised Catherine. Not many people resorted to a foreign language to issue an insult. Nonetheless, she enjoyed her first relaxed smile in more than an hour. Stephen, however, didn't smile. There was nothing teasing or relaxed about his dark gaze when it connected with hers.

"You're a woman to be taken seriously."

They were simple words, issued as a simple statement, and they left her simply staggered.

Late on Friday afternoon, Stephen studied the estimates Catherine had given him as he waited for his cousin to arrive. It was ten to five, and he planned to spend the weekend on his sailboat, so he hoped Derek wouldn't be late.

It surprised him that Derek had formally requested a meeting, and at this time of day besides. His cousin's weekend generally started on Thursday and lasted till Tuesday. And if he wanted to see Stephen he usually just barged into his office unannounced, flattering his way around his secretary if Stephen had asked not to be disturbed. But this time he'd sent word a day in advance, neatly typed on company stationary, no less, that he would like to meet in Stephen's office at five o'clock Friday. He had ensured Stephen's attendance by dangling this intriguing little carrot: he wanted to discuss the future of the company.

Stephen hadn't thought his cousin cared about the department store chain their grandfather's father had founded as much as he cared about the trust fund that kept him in designer suits and Swiss Alps ski vacations. When their grandfather had died two years earlier, he'd left Stephen at the helm of the faltering chain, with Derek second in command. Derek's title was officially vice president, but he generally left the day-to-day operations and all of the crucial decision-making to Stephen and the rest of the management team. He was no intellectual lightweight, but he'd made it clear he wanted the Danbury lifestyle far more than the burden of the legacy.

Stephen closed his eyes and pinched the bridge of his nose, hoping to ward off the headache that was already threatening. The truth was that the struggling department store chain might not be able to ensure Derek's lavish spending much longer without a major turnaround. Marguerite had been making noise about selling in recent months. So far Stephen had been able to block the move. Admittedly, it went beyond pure business for him. He was not about to give up the birthright he was still striving to prove to his dead grandfather he was entitled to.

He figured this meeting would probably be an attempt by Derek to wheedle him around to a sale, so he wasn't surprised when his cousin walked through the door followed by Marguerite. What did surprise him, though, was that they had brought with them the Danburys' longtime family attorney, Lyle Moore.

Stephen sent his aunt a polite smile and motioned toward the small conference table tucked into the corner of his office. Turning to Lyle, he said, "This is unexpected. I didn't know you were coming by today."

The man who had handled everything from Derek's prenuptial agreement to the cousins' trust funds barely spared him a glance. He seemed uncomfortable, nervous, even, and when he finally offered a hand its palm was damp and clammy.

"Can I get anyone a drink?" Stephen asked.

The attorney shook his balding head, and Marguerite declined as well, but Derek flashed a cocky grin. "I'll take one. To celebrate."

Warning bells were going off in Stephen's head, though he couldn't figure out why. But the malicious amusement in Derek's light eyes made him wary.

"You know where it is."

Derek poured himself a brandy at the bar discreetly tucked behind a door in the paneled wall. When he was lounging in his seat, swirling amber liquid in a snifter, Lyle unsnapped the flaps of the overstuffed leather case balanced on his knees and pulled out a document.

He cleared his throat and began, "You've seen this before, of course."

"Grandfather's will." Stephen's stomach knotted.

"Then you know what Sunday is."

"Sunday?"

"It's your birthday," Derek supplied, his grin reminiscent of a shark's. "I never forget it because it comes just one day before mine."

The attorney cleared his throat a second time, and flipped through the papers he'd laid on the table before him.

"Um, as you know, since you are the oldest, your grandfather left you the controlling interest in Danbury's when he died two years ago, with Derek and his mother's portion totaling forty-nine percent of the assets."

"I believe we covered this at the time, Lyle."

"Yes, but the terms of the…um…codicil have not been met."

"Codicil? There was no codicil."

The lawyer ignored him and went on. "Your grandfather felt since you boys were born only one day apart—and you had come a few weeks premature, Stephen—he should make things a little more fair for Derek."

Stephen almost laughed aloud. Fair? His grandfather had always shown a preference for Derek, who looked so much like a Danbury should look, with his golden hair and sky-colored eyes. Stephen favored his mother, a sticking point with the old man, which was why Stephen had been surprised—shocked, even—when the will had been read two years earlier. Despite his obvious bias toward Derek, Maxwell had followed family tradition by giving the oldest Danbury heir control of the family empire. Stephen hadn't been the only one caught off guard. As he recalled his aunt had all but swooned at the time. Derek, however, had seemed to take it all in his stride.

"Your grandfather saw Danbury's as a family business, and he was troubled that neither of his grandsons was married and starting the next generation."

Stephen nearly smiled, remembering the arguments that had often occurred after Sunday dinner, at which some dreamy-eyed debutante or another would have turned up at the table.

"Yes, he believed it should remain a family enterprise, passed from one generation of Danburys to the next," Stephen agreed. Shooting Derek a look, he added, "He didn't want to see the company sold."

The lawyer pulled a pair of reading glasses from his breast pocket and settled them on his nose.

"Yes, well, your grandfather wanted to ensure its future through your and Derek's children. Unfortunately, neither of you has married and produced legitimate heirs at this point."

"So?"

Lyle glanced up nervously, but didn't maintain eye contact. "Well, you know how Maxwell could be. He thought perhaps a little incentive would move things along."

"Just cut to the chase, Lyle," Stephen said impatiently.

Derek's grin broadened. "Yes, Lyle, get to the good part."

"Well, as per the terms of the codicil, if by your thirty-fifth birthdays one of you was legally married, and hopefully but not necessarily on the way to fatherhood, he would inherit not just the controlling interest in Danbury's but all of it, with the exception of the five percent already willed to Marguerite.''

''What are you talking about?''

The lawyer ignored Stephen's outburst and continued.

''If both of you were married the terms of the original will would stand. But if neither of you were married, which is the case, you were to share the remaining ninety-five percent interest in Danbury's equally.''

''That's a lie!'' Stephen's fist pounded the tabletop, followed by an oath.

The lawyer jumped, but he continued in a shaky voice, ''You turn thirty-five on Sunday, Derek on Monday. The codicil states—''

''Let me clarify it for him, Lyle,'' Derek interrupted. He held up his glass of brandy, as if to offer a toast. ''As of Sunday, Mother and I own the controlling interest in Danbury's.''

''Shut up, Derek,'' Stephen said between gritted teeth.

Lyle blotted perspiration from his forehead with a neatly folded handkerchief. ''I'm sure Max didn't add this stipulation to create discord. He was just thinking about the company, and both of you, of course. He wanted to see you married and happy.''

''What Grandfather thought or didn't think is irrelevant. There's no codicil, Lyle, and you damn well know it.'' Standing, he faced the men sitting across from him. One was grinning smugly. The other was swallowing almost convulsively. Next to them his aunt smiled serenely, thanks to the Botox that had paralyzed a good portion of her facial muscles, but nothing could mask the triumph flashing in her eyes.

''It's there in black and white, dear, and signed by Maxwell. I can't believe you could have forgotten about it,'' she said with false sympathy.

''I didn't forget. I have a copy of the will in my safe at home, and there's no codicil. If that codicil is real I was never informed of its existence.''

''Three people in this room remember things differently,'' Derek said.

''I don't know what kind of game the two of you are playing.'' Turning to the attorney, he added, ''And I don't know how they managed to rope you into this. But I'll take this to court if need be.''

''Take it to court.'' Marguerite shrugged. ''Everyone who knows Max will find this to be just the type of thing that controlling old man would do. He was never above using a little high-handed pressure to get his way. Truthfully, I'm surprised you didn't bend to his will. You could easily have ensured a larger inheritance by getting married. You could have married the maid, even. Oh, but that's been done, hasn't it?''

''Leave my mother out of this,'' Stephen warned.

''So defensive.'' Marguerite tsked. ''I didn't mean to dredge up the past. It's just that you were always so pathetically eager to do Maxwell's bidding when he was alive, as if by jumping through all the hoops he set out you could somehow win his approval.'' She pursed a pair of pouty, collagen-filled lips. ''But all he had to do was look at you to know why you weren't an acceptable Danbury heir.''

Stephen pushed aside the old fury and struggled to concentrate on the matter at hand.

''Grandfather would have wanted the company to stay in the family, Lyle. Even assuming this codicil is real, surely you understand what these two barracudas are up to? And you know I was never informed.''

The attorney glanced up, and then away. But before he did, Stephen thought he saw regret and apology in his gaze.

''As Maxwell's attorney, it's not my place to question his motives or what results from them. I'm sorry things did not work out as you would have liked them to, but there's nothing I can do about it. Nothing,'' he repeated on a shaky sigh.

''Fine, this meeting is over, then.'' Stephen stalked to the door, yanked it open and glared back at his cousin and his aunt. ''Danbury's is still mine to run until a court of law says otherwise. And it's not for sale.''

''Don't be so sure. Fieldman's has made another offer,'' Derek replied, naming one of Danbury's most formidable competitors. For a man who rarely stumbled into the office for more than a few hours at a time he was suddenly very well versed in Danbury's financial status, the specifics of the federal bankruptcy code, and just how close Danbury's was coming to having to file for Chapter Eleven.

"Fieldman's wants a bigger slice of the market and it's in a position to pay handsomely to get it. We drag our feet much longer and there will just be bones for the scavengers to fight over. I don't intend to wait that long."

"Danbury's isn't dead yet. The name is solid. It resonates with consumers."

"It resonates with consumers sixty and older, so it might as well be dead. Among eighteen to thirty-five-year-olds we're not even on the radar. That goes double for the under-eighteen market and all their wonderful disposable income."

"We can turn it around. How can you even consider selling out?"

"Money," Derek said succinctly. "I've taken the liberty of setting up a meeting with Fieldman's people on Tuesday. I'm taking Monday off, since it's my birthday and I plan to be celebrating. They're coming to us, ten a.m. sharp. Get used to the idea, cousin. We're going to sell."

"We'll see about that," Stephen replied.

CHAPTER THREE

CATHERINE wasn't sure why she'd come. She could have called Stephen with the additional estimate she'd received on the shelter's roof. As for his robe, which she'd worn home from their evening on *La Libertad,* it could have been sent by messenger. But here she stood, in front of his home in one of Chicago's toniest suburbs, a good forty-minute commute from the city, so she couldn't possibly claim to have been "just in the neighborhood."

She'd been to Stephen's Tudor-style home only a few times, for company management parties he'd hosted while she and Derek were dating. Still, it surprised her to find that he lived on a quiet elm-lined drive where the estates were huge and ivy-covered but still managed to look homey and inviting. Derek lived in the city, in a penthouse apartment high above the throbbing nightlife and bustling streets. She called the city home as well, but she'd always hoped to again live someplace with a rolling green lawn and lush flower gardens to tend.

Catherine grinned when a yellow Labrador retriever streaked down the redbrick drive to greet her as she stepped from her car. She'd always believed she was a dog person at heart, even though her only

pet as a child had been a finicky Persian cat her
mother had named Cashmere.

"Hey, girl," she said, bending down to stroke the
dog's wide head. The Lab instantly dropped to the
ground and rolled over, eager for a belly rub. "Ah,
boy," she amended. "Your master busy?"

Stephen's car was in the circular drive just ahead
of hers. She straightened and started for the rounded
steps of the front porch, noticing for the first time that
that the door was wide open.

"Stephen?"

She got no answer, so she stepped inside. His suit
coat lay crumpled on an oriental rug and it appeared
his briefcase had been tossed onto the long-legged
table in the foyer, knocking off a vase. Shards of glass
littered the marble floor, and she stepped carefully
around them.

Something was wrong, seriously wrong, but almost
immediately she dismissed concern over a burglary or
violent struggle. Surely the dog wouldn't have been
running around outside if his master were in a fight
for his life? From somewhere in the house she could
hear Stephen's raised voice. He was shouting curses,
some in English, some in what sounded like
Spanish—all were vicious.

Catherine called out his name a second time. She
got no answer, but followed his voice down a hallway
and found him in a room she assumed was his home
office. He was quiet now, too quiet, as he sat in a
high-backed leather chair behind an ornately carved

wooden desk, elbows propped on the edge of it, face buried in his hands.

"Stephen?"

He started at the sound of her voice and straightened in his seat. The naked pain in his eyes when he glanced up so surprised her that before she could ponder if he would appreciate her interference or not she was crossing the threshold and walking to him.

"My God, Stephen, what is it? What's wrong?"

"They did it."

"Did what? Who?"

He looked at her, seemed to look through her.

"I don't know how they did it, but they did it." His words clarified nothing. Nor did it help when he motioned to the papers scattered over his desktop and added, "Even my copy of the will, the codicil's there. They must have made the switch last month, when Derek volunteered to pick up some documents for me. I gave him the damn combination to my safe." He swore again. "I all but handed him my birthright."

She didn't know what he was talking about, but that didn't seem as important at that moment as offering comfort. She walked around the desk, laid a hand on his shoulder.

"How can I help? What can I do?"

"There's nothing you can do." He laughed harshly.

"There must be something."

He shook his head, as if realizing for the first time who she was. "Why are you here, Catherine?"

She decided against mentioning the shelter's roof. He obviously had more pressing concerns right now. So she pointed to the shopping bag she'd left just inside the door. "Your robe. I'm returning it."

"Leave it, then."

It was a dismissal, but she decided to ignore it.

"What can I do?" she asked again.

He didn't answer. Instead he stood, and with a violent sweep of his arm cleared the desk. A lamp crashed to the ground, followed by a telephone, and papers fluttered like snowflakes before finally settling on the hardwood floor.

Catherine jumped back a step, shocked by Stephen's uncharacteristic show of temper. In an instant he seemed to have gone from distraught to enraged. And in those dark eyes of his she saw fury, burning hot and lethal. And his gaze was now focused on her.

"It seems we have something in common, Catherine."

He rolled the R in her name, making it sound almost exotic. She backed up another step as he advanced, not sure what he meant to do. When he stood directly in front of her he raised a hand, and she held her breath. But his touch was gentle when he pushed the hair back from her face and tucked it behind her ear, his fingers sliding slowly down to the end of the strand before releasing it.

"What do we have in common?" she asked softly.

"Betrayal. Derek has betrayed us both."

He cursed again, before turning away from her and stalking to the window.

"I don't understand."

"Derek and his mother managed to either doctor our grandfather's will or conceal a key provision of it from me until today." He turned and pointed to the papers scattered over the floor. "There's a codicil that essentially gives them the controlling interest in Danbury's if certain conditions aren't met by my thirty-fifth birthday, which is Sunday."

"Any chance you can meet the conditions?"

He expelled a breath, ran one hand through his hair. Fury ebbed. He seemed resigned when he replied. "It's not likely."

"Okay, but surely you could go to court and challenge the will?"

"Perhaps. I'd need a new lawyer, since they seem to have bought off the one who's been doing our family's business for decades. It would get ugly," he said, as if thinking aloud. "And there's no guarantee I'd win, since I have no proof that they concealed the codicil. It's their word against mine. In the months or even years before the matter is finally settled the press would have a field day with the story, as would our competitors. I wonder what such a bitter battle would do to Danbury's already battered bottom line in the end?"

"I'd say your best option, then, is to try to meet the will's conditions."

He snorted. "Easier said than done."

"If you don't mind me asking, what are the conditions?"

"I have to be married," he announced. Glancing at his watch, he added, "And I have less than twenty-eight hours to do so."

"That's archaic—barbaric."

"That's my grandfather. Which is why I tend to think the codicil is authentic. Derek must have discovered it before Grandfather died and decided to make sure I didn't know about it until it was too late. I still can't figure out how he and his mother bought off Lyle. He's always seemed so by the book."

Something occurred to her then, a thought too hideous to even consider, and yet she had to know. "This condition, did it apply to Derek?"

He seemed to understand what she was asking. "I'm sorry, Catherine."

She acknowledged his apology with a brisk nod, as hurt and fury battled for dominance. Derek's words at the church came back to her. *I don't really need her anyway.* Had everything been a lie?

She recalled her first encounter with Derek, nearly two years earlier—just a month after his grandfather's death, she now realized. He'd bid an outrageous sum for a mediocre painting at a silent auction she'd organized to raise money for the shelter. She'd thanked him personally afterward, accepting his invitation to dinner the next day. She'd thought at last she'd found someone who shared her interests, respected her intellect and understood the importance of her work at the shelter and with other local charities that helped serve the city's neediest residents. Had his romantic pursuit really just been a means to an end?

"What would have happened if Derek had married me?" she asked in a quiet voice.

"That's not important."

"Don't try to spare my feelings, Stephen. I think I have a right to know. What would have happened?"

"He would have had it all."

"All of Danbury's?"

"Everything." His gaze skimmed her features in a way that made her breath catch. "And then some."

She thought about the prenuptial agreement she'd signed, ensuring a reasonable cash settlement but stipulating she would have no part of the family business. He would have had everything, all right.

"But without a wife he still wins, since you are unmarried as well?"

"Not as neatly. We'll technically have an equal interest in Danbury's. His mother's five percent, however, will mean they get to call the shots. And they intend to sell."

"So he would have married me just to get his hands on Danbury's." She shifted her gaze to Stephen. "Would you?"

"Excuse me?"

"Would you marry someone to keep the company?"

He snorted out a laugh. "I'm not even seeing any-one."

"That didn't stop Derek."

"No, but he had time on his side. I've got just over a day. I'm not a believer in love at first sight."

"You don't have to love her," she said, the cold truth settling in once and for all. "Derek didn't love me."

"He should have."

His tone was so matter-of-fact that she didn't doubt he believed it.

An idea began to take form, too outrageous to entertain, let alone voice, and yet she heard herself ask, "What kind of wife does the codicil state you need to have?"

He stared at her blankly for a moment, before shrugging. "The usual kind: female."

"Are there any restrictions? Do you have to…stay married?"

"No, I guess not." His brows pulled together. "But marriage should be permanent."

His tone sounded almost wistful, and the words surprised her. Stephen Danbury seemed too much of a realist to be a romantic. But then her judgment of men was hardly reliable. After all, she'd believed the lies Derek had packaged up and delivered. But he'd never loved her. He'd never intended to honor or cherish her. He hadn't even been capable of fidelity on their wedding day. And for his deceit he would have reaped huge rewards. Even having been caught he was still about to come out on top.

It wasn't fair. It wasn't right.

"You could marry me." Catherine laid a hand over her jack-hammering heart after she said it.

Stephen gaped at her, clearly as surprised as she by the suggestion. "Marry you?"

Self-conscious laughter bubbled to the surface. "You needn't look so horrified. It's just an idea."

Stephen came forward until he stood just in front of her. "I'm not horrified, just surprised. I know what I'd get out of a marriage between us," he said carefully, "but what about you? What would you get out of it?"

"I'm not expecting anything financially. I do earn a salary at the shelter, and I have some money from a small inheritance my grandmother left me."

"I didn't think you were after money, otherwise you would have married Derek even after finding him with the wedding planner. But why would you want to marry me?"

Helping people. That was what she did. She often put herself on the line for the underdog, albeit never quite so personally. And then there was the way her pulse hitched whenever he looked at her in that intense way of his. But attraction alone was no reason to marry. Why was she willing to do this? She had no answer for herself, certainly none for him. So she settled on, "It's for a good cause."

"The shelter?" he asked. "Is this your way to ensure you get that new roof?"

"Will it?"

Something flickered in his gaze, an emotion she couldn't quite read. "Consider it done."

"Thank you. But this isn't just about the shelter." She fussed with the mother-of-pearl buttons on her sweater set and admitted, "I'm afraid I'm not as altruistic as that."

His lips thinned into a smile. "Let me guess: this would be your way of paying Derek back? A little bit of revenge from the woman scorned?."

She nodded. "I suppose that's true. As much as I want the good guy in all of this to win, I'd also like to see the bad guy lose."

"Are you sure I'm the good guy, Catherine?"

His gaze locked with hers in seeming challenge.

"I want you to be," she whispered.

"Why?"

She gave a nervous laugh. "Yin and Yang, I suppose. One to balance out the other."

"So you'd marry me to keep the cosmic forces in order?"

She didn't reply. In a way it had to do with cosmic forces, all right, but not necessarily the ones he assumed. For the first time in her life Catherine was handing herself over to fate. This was the right thing to do. She could feel it, even if she couldn't articulate why.

"If we do this, we'll need to do it quickly and quietly," Stephen said.

"You'll marry me, then?"

Stephen studied Catherine's face. There was no denying her beauty. It had long beguiled him, even when he hadn't thought there was much else to her than physical perfection. Under other circumstances he might have been flattered by the proposal. Under other circumstances, however, he knew it would not have come. Women from Catherine's elite social sphere might condescend to take a dip in Stephen's gene pool, but they didn't want to swim there forever. Years of dating had told him so, despite his fortune.

"I'm desperate, Catherine," he said flatly.

He watched her wince and wondered was he so desperate he would take a wife, even if only on paper? He didn't have the luxury of time to clearly think things out. The one thing he knew without hesitation or question was that he did not want to see Danbury's sold. Marrying Catherine might be his only way to stop that from happening.

"Is that a yes?"

He nodded. "We'll need to move fast. Danbury's no longer has a company jet. The bottom line has been too thin in recent years to justify it. We'll have to catch a flight out of O'Hare."

"A flight?"

"Vegas." He shrugged. "It's quick and legal."

"Vegas," she repeated, looking as if she were sucking on a sour ball.

"You don't have to do this."

She moved forward, offering her hand as she came. "I do."

And it was with just those two words that she sealed the bargain.

It was nearly midnight when they arrived in Las Vegas. The city, however, seemed to have an abundance of energy and enthusiasm despite the late hour. Catherine had neither, especially since she was still working on Illinois time. She had never been to Vegas. She wasn't one for games of chance, which of course seemed ironic given the risk she would be taking with Stephen. For a woman who didn't believe in gambling, she'd certainly found herself in a high-stakes game.

What did she know about this man who would soon become her husband? Not much. Not nearly enough for the commitment she had agreed to make. He was private, but it was more than that. He hid something—not something evil, like Derek, of that she was sure. But those eyes that watched everything and rarely reflected anything told her that he found it easier—safer?—to tuck his feelings deep inside. She could appreciate that, she thought. She'd done it most of her life when it came to her parents.

"Tired?"

The softly spoken question startled her. She turned from the cab's window to find him staring at her. "No. Not really. I've never been to Las Vegas."

He studied her for a moment longer before replying, "It's not really your style."

"How can you be so sure?" She found herself a

little bothered that, while he seemed such an enigma to her, he should consider her such an open book.

"It's gaudy, flashy, at times crass and always greedy. You are conservative, traditional, sedate...generous."

"That's just how every woman wants to be described by her prospective groom. You might as well be talking about a station wagon," she said on a nervous laugh, but she wasn't really insulted.

He only raised one ebony eyebrow, and she found herself lost in those dark eyes. *How does he see me?*

"Try again," she said, turning in her seat so that she fully faced him.

"You have style," he said slowly.

"Hmm. Now I'm a Mercedes."

But she didn't laugh this time. She could scarcely breathe when he looked at her like that, his gaze so thorough, as if no detail could escape his notice.

"You're beautiful, but you know that."

"It's often an empty compliment," she replied.

"Which brings me to smart, but I suspect you know that, too."

She shrugged. "Well, it's not something I hear often from men."

Despite her outward nonchalance, genuine pleasure had her pulse spiking. Men so rarely complimented her on her intelligence. Oh, she was no genius, but neither was she a vapid member of the social elite. She had graduated *cum laude* from Stanford University, with a dual degree in business and social work. She put both disciplines to work in her job at the shelter. She enjoyed the work immensely, which was why she also volunteered her services at half a dozen other charities. She was a natural at fund-raising and organizing, and it made her feel useful rather than like some pretty ornament.

It also helped ease her guilt. Once upon a time she had been useless. Her best friend had paid the price. She pushed back that painful memory as the driver pulled the car to a stop in front of their hotel.

They had each only brought one small case to spare them from checking luggage, but Stephen insisted on carrying hers. Inside, it seemed ridiculous to request separate rooms when they were in town to be married, but Catherine wondered how she could sleep in the same proximity as Stephen, share a bathroom, when they had never so much as gone on a date. The dilemma was solved to a certain extent when he requested a suite. Their quarters were opulently decorated in navy and gold, and spacious enough with two bedrooms, each with its own bath.

"Which room do you want?" he asked politely as they stood in the living area and eyed one another with growing discomfort.

"Doesn't matter. I'm so tired I could sleep standing up." She laughed, hoping to lighten the mood. He didn't so much as blink.

"You can take that one." He pointed to the doorway nearest her. He hesitated at the threshold of the other bedroom, carry-on bag in hand. "Thank you, Catherine."

She nodded, not trusting herself to speak.

"Try to get some sleep. We have a big day ahead of us."

As Catherine settled between the cool sheets of the king-sized bed, she knew "big" was an understatement.

Early the next morning they picked a chapel within walking distance from their hotel, opting for what passed for understated in Las Vegas. Plastic blood-red roses dripped from a white trellis just outside the door, and inside the lobby guests could put a buck in a vending machine to buy a packet of birdseed to toss at the bride and groom.

Of course there were no guests: only Catherine, wearing a simple white A-line dress that flowed nearly to her ankles, and Stephen, dressed in a charcoal suit. She supposed it was silly to wear white for this farce of a wedding, but she believed in tradition.

A Vegas wedding, she soon realized, had traditions of its own, quirkiness being at the top of the list. They managed to bypass the Elvis impersonator, but to Catherine's horrified amusement, the I Do Chapel's minister bore a striking resemblance to Liberace.

"The standard wedding package includes your choice of song, a bouquet of white carnations for the bride and a snapshot to remember the happy occasion," Liberace droned. "For just a little more you can upgrade to the deluxe package and get the pretty little lady a bouquet of roses, three snapshots and these matching T-shirts.''

He pointed to the wall where the shirts were displayed. Emblazoned on the front of each were the words "We did it in Vegas at the I Do Chapel.''

"Oh, my God,'' Catherine gasped, swallowing a bubble of hysterical laughter.

To her surprise, Stephen said dryly, "The deluxe package, by all means. We wouldn't want to miss out on those shirts.''

The entire affair seemed so out of character for both of them, she supposed they would need the T-shirts to convince themselves they'd actually gone through with it. Of course, the marriage certificate would be real enough. That thought was sobering.

After filling out the necessary paperwork, they followed Liberace into the main room of the chapel.

"Are you expecting any guests?''

"No,'' Stephen said.

"Then I guess we'll get down to it.''

Before Catherine could catch a breath, a woman shoved a bouquet of plastic white roses into her hands and snapped a hasty shot of her and Stephen as they stood before a makeshift altar. Liberace nodded to another woman, who cued up the music. "Greensleeves'' filled the room.

"Dearly beloved,'' Liberace began, speaking to a room occupied by only five people, including the bride and groom. "We are gathered here today to unite this woman and this man in matrimony. Do you…?'' He glanced at the paper before him and then back at Stephen. ''I'm sorry. Could you pronounce your name for me, please?''

Stephen nodded, but his gaze never left Catherine's face as he replied, ''Stefano Anastasio Danbury.''

The name rolled from his tongue, a perfect complement to the dark hair and eyes—eyes that now stared in challenge, as if daring her to comment, and so she did.

''I wondered what the A stood for.''

Something like surprise flickered briefly in his expression. Clearly this was not the comment he was expecting.

''My grandparents—paternal grandparents—preferred it that way.''

Catherine had never met the elder Danburys, but she thought she understood what he was saying. Stefano would have been easy enough to Anglicize, but a name like Anastasio would have no English equivalent. She wasn't one to pay attention to the gossip, but she now recalled that she'd heard her mother talking to a friend once about a scandal of some sort, involving Stephen's father and the woman he'd married.

''Your mother was from Puerto Rico,'' she said, pleased with herself for finally remembering. It made sense to her now that he would have learned her native tongue.

"My mother was a maid," he said flatly. "No other comment?"

"Your initials spell SAD."

His brows tugged together.

"May I continue?" the minister asked.

"That's up to the lady," Stephen replied.

Did he expect her to call it off just because his name confirmed the heritage his looks hinted at?

"Is there suddenly a reason I shouldn't want to?" She lobbed the ball neatly back into his court. If he thought her a bigot, let him spell it out.

"You have every reason in the world not to want to."

"Those reasons were the same back in Chicago. Exactly the same," she enunciated. "I haven't changed my mind. Have you?"

"I'm beginning to wonder if I've lost my mind, but, no, I haven't changed it." He nodded to Liberace. "Proceed."

The ceremony was over in short order. A couple of "I dos," the exchange of two hastily purchased gold bands from chapel's display case—guaranteed not to tarnish for at least five years—and they were pronounced Mr. and Mrs. Stefano Danbury.

"You may kiss your bride."

Catherine hadn't allowed herself to think ahead to this part of the ceremony, or, for that matter, to the physical side of marriage. Of course their marriage would be in name only, a marriage of convenience. Wasn't that, to all intents and purposes, what her parents had? A useful and mutually beneficial union. They seemed content enough after twenty-nine years. Yoked together. Like a pair of oxen.

Of course she and Stephen were hardly in this for the long haul. They'd settled on a year, which seemed a reasonable enough length of time to silence the gossips and satisfy any lawyers Derek hired to fight the codicil or question their nuptials. Something told Catherine that her marriage to Derek would have ended much sooner and far less amicably than she predicted this one would.

Her gaze connected with Stephen's. For better or worse, literally, he was her husband now. She offered a smile, leaned forward for the kiss, expecting something brief and perfunctory. Then she caught the clean scent of aftershave on his warm skin, noted the sexy line of his mouth. Reaching up, she laid a palm against the hard plain of one of his cheeks, and, for no reason she could fathom, she sighed.

Stephen saw her eyelids flutter shut as his mouth touched hers, but he kept his own eyes open, watching this woman he barely knew, watching his wife. He deepened the kiss out of curiosity, sliding his tongue inside the pliant seam of her lips. She'd always seemed so cool, so in control. Once, a few months back, he'd walked into Derek's office and caught the pair of them kissing. Even with his cousin's hand on her nicely curved bottom and her arms twined around his neck she'd managed to look untouched. She didn't look untouched this time, though he'd so far managed to keep his hands to himself. And neither, he admitted, was he. Kissing Catherine was like sailing *La Libertad* in rough waters. He needed to hold on. He brought his hands up to frame her face, his fingers stretching into the soft gold of her hair.

"That's more like it," Liberace cracked. "Now, if you kids could just take this back to your hotel room, I've got another wedding to perform. Don't forget to pick up your T-shirts on the way out."

They sprung apart as if they had just been doused with a bucketful of freezing water. Her eyes, as big and blue as the deepest waters of Lake Michigan, reflected his own surprise and confusion. An electrical current of need had coursed through that kiss. It had carried with it a blast of heat that he hadn't felt in…ever. And it had come from the Ice Princess, Catherine Canton. The discovery, however, was not welcome. Business. That was what this was, Stephen reminded himself. Hormones didn't, *couldn't* factor into it. Even as he told himself this was so, he couldn't quite squelch the male satisfaction he felt when he noted the way her hand shook when she ran it through her hair. She'd worn her hair loose and long this day, a cascade of sunshine that haloed her face and flowed over her shoulders. He liked it this way the best, especially since the slightly mussed tendrils around her temples had been his doing.

The photographer handed Stephen the three Polaroids, which he stuffed into his pocket without bothering to look at them. They were nearly to the door, his equilibrium almost restored, when Liberace ruined it all by calling out, "Enjoy your wedding night."

CHAPTER FOUR

IN THE glaring sun, Las Vegas didn't have quite the high-voltage impact it did at night. But, sheened in a gaudy kind of glamour, it still throbbed with excitement.

Catherine wanted nothing more than a few minutes to herself, to try to put that searing kiss into perspective. She tried to be analytical about it. Could her reaction merely have been the desperate need for sexual validation by woman recently rejected? Perhaps, but that did little to cool her blood. This was the desert, but where had all that heat come from? She hadn't known a simple kiss could be like that, shooting a million flaming arrows of need through her system, each one of them unerringly finding its mark.

"What now?"

She hadn't meant to ask the question aloud, as it was more rhetorical than anything else, but Stephen answered.

"We can play tourist for a few hours, if you'd like. Our flight doesn't leave till this evening. Ever play poker?"

It seemed like such an outrageous thing to do just after getting married that she couldn't help but smile. "Once, at a Vegas night a literacy program held to raise money for supplies. Five-card stud, or something like that.''

"Well, your money wouldn't go for a good cause this time."

"How do you know I'll lose?" she asked, fascinated by the gold flecks the sun had teased out of his otherwise dark eyes.

"Odds favor the house."

"I don't like those odds."

He shrugged. "Every now and then someone hits it big. That's gambling's allure, the potential for winning the jackpot. That's why some people bet their life savings and then some."

"It makes sense that we're here, then."

"Why do you say that?"

"You just bet on me, gambled with your legacy."

"No, I'd already lost my legacy. I had nothing to lose. That's the first rule of gambling, by the way: don't bet more than you can afford to lose."

"I guess Derek doesn't know that rule."

"No. But then Derek doesn't care about his legacy either. He's about to lose. Big time."

Catherine couldn't help but wonder if they had won or if they, too, would find themselves paying once everything was said and done.

Their flight home was the flight from hell. Delayed nearly two hours, and then rocked by turbulence, it seemed to last an eternity. A superstitious woman would have considered it a bad omen. White-knuckled and terrified, Catherine merely endured it as best she could. Beside her, Stephen slept like a baby.

To keep her mind off her nerves, she studied his features: the sensual line of his lips; the square jaw that was now shadowed and in need of a shave; the thick, dark hair that had fallen over his brow. In sleep he looked oddly vulnerable, and incredibly sexy. She recalled their kiss and felt her face grow warm. People called her an ice princess. She pressed her head back, stared at the ''fasten seatbelt'' sign and sucked in several calming breaths before closing her eyes. What would they say if they could read her mind just now?

''Penny for your thoughts?''

Her eyelids snapped open. Turning her head she found herself nearly nose to nose with Stephen.

They both straightened in their seats.

''I didn't mean to startle you. I just wondered what you were thinking. You looked so…intense.''

She forced a laugh. ''I don't care to fly.''

''Do the deep-breathing exercises help?'' he asked.

She met his dark gaze, felt her heart tremble, and said with conviction, ''Not one bit.''

It was well past midnight when they finally touched down at O'Hare. Glitzy Vegas had cocooned them in illusion. Gritty Chicago doused them in reality. They were husband and wife on what could still be called their wedding night, and yet they were stuck in all of the awkwardness of a first date.

"I'll take you home," he said, as if they had just gone to dinner and caught a movie.

"I can grab a cab," Catherine replied. "It's out of your way."

"I'll take you home. You can get your things."

"My things?"

"You're my wife, Catherine. You will live with me."

His tone offered no room for negotiation, let alone contradiction. Still, she heard herself say, "But I thought…" And then her voice trailed away.

Actually, she had not thought about their living arrangements at all. There simply hadn't been time during their mad dash to the altar.

"You'll have your own room, if that's your concern. I don't expect a physical relationship."

"I'll have my own room," she repeated, still feeling dazed. But Stephen must have taken her words to mean she was questioning his sincerity.

"I don't expect you to sleep with me, Catherine. We needn't consummate our marriage to make it look real to others. Living together should accomplish that."

Despite his assurances, her mind conjured up a vivid mental picture of them locked together in passion. She couldn't imagine where this inappropriate visual had come from, but at the moment the only question on her mind was: what kind of lover would Stephen be? That kiss made her wonder. Still waters, she thought. He'd be one to pay attention to detail.

To dot every i and cross every t. She licked her dry lips.

"There's no reason to be nervous," he said. "Despite my *hot Latin blood*, I can be a perfect gentleman when it is required."

His words were mocking, but she thought he sounded insulted as well.

"I'm not nervous, Stephen. I trust you."

He took the carry-on bag from her hand and started toward the exits. And she would have sworn she heard him reply, "Maybe you shouldn't."

The dog offered up a loud and enthusiastic greeting, his tail slicing through the air like a pirate's sword, when Stephen pushed open the door that led from the garage into the house. Stephen had asked a neighbor to come by to see to the dog's needs while he was away, but the Lab acted as if he'd been in solitary confinement for months.

"That's enough, Degas." He patted the dog's wide head. "Let's show some manners, shall we? There's someone I want you to meet. Sit."

The hound obediently plopped his hind end down on the floor, his tongue lolling out.

Turning to Catherine, Stephen said, "This is Degas. He's harmless enough, but he sheds a lot, so you might want to keep your distance. Or not," he added when Catherine, unmindful of her black linen pantsuit, bent down on one knee to give the dog an affectionate pat. Degas presented her with his paw, which she shook.

"We met the other day." When his eager tongue washed her face, she added, "I think he likes me."

She sounded as excited as a kid, and unbothered by the fact she'd just been slobbered on by a dog. *What's not to like?* he thought, and felt the same unmistakable surge of attraction he'd felt when he'd kissed her. Had that really only been mere hours ago? It seemed as if a lifetime had passed.

Need made his voice gruff when he said, "Come on, I'll show you to your room."

She followed him through the darkened house, wondering why he suddenly seemed so remote. Even the dog was more subdued as he walked beside her, as if he too sensed his master's sudden mood shift.

He flipped on a couple of lights as he walked, but their glow appeared to do nothing to brighten his mood. When he reached the staircase, he turned to take her carry-on case, even though he already had her suitcase. Then, without a word, he started up.

Their footsteps were muffled by a dark tapestry runner, and she wondered who had done his decorating. He'd hired it out, she was sure of it. It was certainly tasteful, with shades of navy and taupe carried throughout, but it seemed staid and lacking in warmth, just like the man himself at the moment.

Catherine missed the bright French country décor with which she'd decorated her apartment. When she and Derek had become engaged he'd persuaded her that they should live in his penthouse after their marriage and keep his modern furnishings, which complemented the high walls of windows and steeply angled ceilings. So she'd donated her sofa, chairs, coffee table, lamps, even her lovely Duncan Fife dining room set, to a charity auction. She'd come home on her non-wedding night to little more than a mattress on the floor, the sleigh bed having been disposed of as well.

"Is anything wrong?" Stephen asked.

"Nothing. It's not important."

He stopped at the top of the stairs. "Tell me."

"I just realized that it's a good thing I sold most of my furniture before my wed—in July. I don't have much to move now."

"Whatever you want to bring to my house I'll make room for. I'll hire movers first thing tomorrow."

Brisk, efficient, impersonal. They were discussing their living arrangements, and yet they might as well have been discussing the weather.

He turned to the right. The upstairs, she realized, was broken into two wings, separated by a long hall that offered a view of the great room below.

"I think you'll find this room acceptable. If you need more closet space, the room next to it also has a walk-in."

He opened the door, and all Catherine saw was the queen-sized bed. Liberace's words came back. This was their wedding night. Or it had been. Now, it was after midnight and they were back to being two strangers, albeit two strangers who shared a last name.

"Goodnight, Catherine."

"It's morning," she pointed out, and then smiled as a thought occurred to her. "And it's your birthday. Happy birthday, Stephen."

She reached out and squeezed his hand, but when she would have let go he held on, using it to draw her closer.

"You looked beautiful today, by the way."

Her heart fluttered ridiculously at the compliment.

"It wasn't a designer original this time."

"It didn't need to be."

He leaned down, hovered for a moment as if in indecision. Finally, he kissed her cheek.

"Should you need anything, my room is the first one to the left of the stairs."

"See you in the morning," she said.

She closed the door and then stood there with her hand on the knob, wondering about the man she had just married. Wondering if they would be friends when their year ended and they went their separate ways. Wondering how she was going to explain her hasty nuptials to her family, and what the press would have to say. Wondering if she'd just made the mistake of a lifetime.

And wondering why, despite all of her concerns, she felt an undeniable shimmer of excitement.

Stephen was not home when Catherine awoke the following morning. It was barely half past nine, and yet when she followed the scent of coffee to the kitchen she found only a note.

> I'll contact the movers today. Coffee might be a little strong for your taste. There's cream in the fridge and sugar in the cupboard next to the stove. S.

Hardly a love letter, she thought, bemused.

After her first eye-opening sip of coffee, she decided to take him up on the offer of cream. Then, leaning back against the cupboard, she glanced around the kitchen. It was a generously proportioned room, with state-of-the-art stainless steel appliances, dark cherry cabinets, and a built-in nook with bench seating. A large window over the sink looked out into a beautifully landscaped yard. The room was functional and yet somehow looked cozy. She decided she liked it best of any room in the house.

"You must be Catherine."

Startled, she turned and found a woman of about sixty standing in the doorway. She wore a dark uniform dress that zipped up the front, and she held a couple of grocery bags, which she now set on the butcher-block island. Catherine had detected a lyrical cadence to her voice when she spoke and, based on her dark coloring, she decided the woman's native tongue was Spanish.

"Yes, hello. I didn't realize anyone was here."

"I'm Rosaria. I let myself in. Stephen called this morning and asked if I would pick up some groceries. I try to keep the kitchen stocked with good food." She winked. "Stephen, he likes…" She seemed to search for a word, then broke into a broad grin. "Junk."

"Junk?"

"You know." She pointed to the refrigerator. "Meals that come from a freezer. He says he doesn't have time to fuss with dinner."

Something seemed obscene about having a kitchen a gourmet would be proud to own and heating up pre-cooked dinners in the microwave.

"You're pretty." She made a little humming noise. "And so thin."

"Thank you," Catherine replied, not sure how else to respond to what might not have been a compliment.

"You're not Stephen's usual type."

"Oh?"

She motioned toward Catherine's hair. "Blonde. I don't know that I ever remember seeing him with a blonde woman before."

"I see." Which, of course, she didn't.

"Of course, I didn't think Stephen would ever marry. He used to say as much whenever I'd tell him that a woman would make good use of this kitchen and all the fancy appliances he had put in here. 'Men can cook, too,' he'd say. But he never bothered to. And no wonder. It's no fun cooking for one."

She put away the groceries as she spoke.

"You look hungry."

"I am, yes," Catherine agreed. "I was just trying to figure out what to make for breakfast."

"Dishes are in the those cabinets." Rosaria pointed. "I brought eggs, and a nice fresh loaf of bread. I could make you an omelet, if you'd like. I've got a few minutes before I have to leave."

"I can do it, but thanks."

"Well, I'll be going, then. Nice to have met you, Catherine." The woman stopped in the doorway. "It's not my place, I know, but Stephen is a good man. He deserves happiness, and there hasn't been a lot of it in his life. I hope you will make him happy."

It wasn't a lie when Catherine replied, "I hope we'll both be happy."

She spent the Sunday doing something she rarely did: puttering. She figured she would play it safe and stay out of sight for the day. Then she put away the belongings she had brought with her and walked around her new home, trying to picture spending all her evenings and weekends there with Stephen. Degas followed her every step.

"What does he do to unwind?" she asked the dog. The words seemed to echo from the vaulted ceilings. "Is he a night owl, a morning person? Does he work late? What does he do most weekends?"

The dog nuzzled her hand, looking for an ear-rub.

"You're about as talkative as your master."

There was a lot she didn't know about her husband, and his house, tastefully decorated as it was, revealed little. At the top of the stairs she turned left instead of right. One room remained to be explored. One room that might shed light on Stephen's personality.

Catherine hesitated only for a moment before turning the knob. This wasn't like her at all, invading someone's privacy, but she couldn't seem to stop herself from stepping over the threshold and into what was aptly named the master bedroom.

The walls were painted a vibrant red, set off by thick white trim at the windows and tall white baseboards. Other bits of color were splashed around the room, and she couldn't help but think he had saved all of it for this room, for so much of the rest of the house was done in less vivid hues.

She spied a photo on his nightstand and, though she had intended to venture no farther inside the room, she found herself crossing to it. It was his parents. She would stake her life on it. She sat on the edge of Stephen's unmade bed and studied the people in the picture. His father had certainly been handsome, with hair just a couple of shades darker than Catherine's and eyes as blue as a summer sky. But it was from his mother that Stephen had inherited his striking looks: the dark eyes, the fuller lips, the prominent cheekbones and slightly flared nose. His mother's eyes held secrets as well, but her smile was warm and inviting.

The dog whined from the doorway. She glanced over and her heart began to pound. Stephen stood there, his expression unreadable, although she had a good idea what he must be thinking.

"Curiosity satisfied, Catherine?"

"I'm sorry. I have no business being in here."

"None," he agreed. "Unless you'd care to change the rules of our marriage?"

He advanced, and she felt her mouth go dry.

"You'll find my bed comfortable and me... accommodating."

She stood. "I'm sorry. I think I should leave."

"Come now, don't tell me you've never wondered if all the talk about Latin men is true?"

"I'd like to think I'm above that kind of immature speculation," she replied stiffly.

"Does ice flow through your veins, Catherine?"

He rolled the R, and then he said something else in Spanish. The musical cadence of the foreign words made understanding them superfluous. And if there were ice in her veins it surely would have melted when he reached out to caress her cheek.

"Why are you doing this?"

"Doing what? Touching my wife?" He took another step forward and placed both hands on her hips.

"Stephen, I..."

"You're curious, Catherine. Admit it."

"All right, yes. I'll admit it. I'm curious about you. I don't think that should come as any surprise. We're married and we're going to be living together."

"I think it goes beyond that. I think you're curious about this."

Stephen intended the kiss to be punishing, but she responded to his boldness with surprising acceptance, shifting her position until their bodies touched from shoulder to thigh. He'd started out as the seducer and wound up feeling seduced, but his voice was steady when he said.

"I think you should go, *querida*. Before we do something that you'll regret."

CHAPTER FIVE

STEPHEN hadn't asked Catherine to attend the meeting Tuesday morning that Derek had scheduled with Fieldman's top brass. He'd mentioned it to her, of course, but not with the expectation that she would be there, especially after that fiasco in his bedroom. He simply wanted her prepared, in case Derek or some tabloid reporter called to confirm her marriage to Stephen. As of yet, word had not leaked out. So it shocked him tremendously when she walked through the door to his office fifteen minutes before nine o'clock. She looked fresh and lovely in a tailored silk suit the color of rich cream, her hair swept back and held in a pearl clip at the nape of her neck. He immediately wished she'd worn it loose.

"I hope I'm not late," she said, casting Stephen a rueful glance. Then she smiled brilliantly before adding, "I haven't been getting much sleep lately, so I'm afraid I didn't hear the alarm go off."

Derek and Marguerite had just settled into their chairs, sipping coffee, clearly pleased with themselves. At Catherine's arrival Derek bobbled his beverage, sending a good portion of it down the front of his snowy shirt.

"What are you doing here?" he asked, scowling

as he tried to mop up the mess. "We have an important meeting in just a few minutes. Anything you want to discuss with me will have to wait until later."

"Yes, dear," Marguerite said, trying to work up a look of sympathy on her frozen face. "It's really poor form to chase after a man, especially one who has made it pretty clear he doesn't want you."

Catherine ignored her, addressing Derek instead. "I'm not here to see you."

"You're here to see Stephen?" He laughed, as if she'd just delivered the punchline of a joke. "Well, that will have to wait until after our meeting, too."

"She stays," Stephen said, pulling out a seat for her.

"Stephen, really, whatever game you two have concocted, it's in poor taste," Marguerite replied. She motioned to their attorney, who had just entered the room, lugging his briefcase. "This is business, not an ice cream social. Fieldman's people will be here any moment."

"My wife stays," Stephen said succinctly, and had the pleasure of watching three mouths drop open.

Derek surged to his feet. "Wife? What do you mean, wife? When did this happen?"

"Saturday, in Las Vegas. You know, cousin, the place where fortunes are won…and lost?"

"You married her?" Marguerite looked suddenly pale.

"You won't get away with this," Derek said.

"I believe that was my line last week. Try to be original."

"Lyle, say something," Marguerite snapped.

The attorney smiled, relief flooding his expression, and offered a hand. "Congratulations, Stephen."

Marguerite swatted his arm. "Don't be a fool, Lyle. Congratulations aren't in order. Don't you see what he's doing? He only married Catherine out of spite. Surely there's something we can do."

"If the marriage is legal, there's nothing. Under the terms of the codicil, Stephen now owns ninety-five percent of Danbury's."

"But that's not fair," Marguerite had the gall to say.

"You still have your five percent," Lyle reminded her. "And Derek is hardly a pauper. He has other assets, although he may not be able to live quite so lavishly from now on."

"You haven't heard the last of this," Derek fumed, as he and Marguerite headed to the door.

When they were gone the room was silent for a moment, then Lyle sank into a chair and grinned. "I can't tell you how happy I am for you, Stephen."

"But last week you stood with them. You claimed I knew about the codicil."

"I never claimed that. Marguerite did. I just never corrected her, for which I'm sorry." His expression sobered. "They can be very persuasive, Stephen. My son had a little trouble a few years back, a gambling debt. A very large one to the wrong people, if you know what I mean. I engaged in some overbilling to gather enough to pay it off.''

''Why didn't you just come to me?''

''I should have. I was ashamed. Keith's not a bad kid, and he's turned his life around. But in trying to help him I broke the law. Derek found out about it somehow, and he used it to find out what Maxwell was planning in his will. When he learned about the codicil he blackmailed me to keep it from you until it was too late.''

''But it wasn't too late.''

''No. Derek wanted to gloat.'' Lyle smiled again when he added, ''His Achilles' heel.''

''And I made the most of it.''

''It obviously never occurred to him that you would beat him at his sleazy game.''

The lawyer shifted uncomfortably after he said it, apparently realizing the unintentional insult his words contained. Glancing at Catherine, he said, ''My apologies, Mrs. Danbury, that came out wrong.''

''An understandable mistake,'' she replied graciously, even as Stephen watched the color stain her cheeks.

''My congratulations and best wishes to both of you.''

''Thank you,'' she said.

The other man fiddled with the handle of his briefcase for a moment, then cleared his throat. To Stephen, he said, ''I'll be resigning as your legal counsel, and I'll understand if you want to take action against me, legally or with the bar.''

Stephen was quiet for a moment, considering. ''I have no plans to do either. As you know, that pair tends to bring out the worst in people. I'd appreciate the name of a good firm, though.''

Lyle's face brightened. ''I know one of the senior partners at Rockwell, Martin, Stanwood. It's an old and respectable firm. I can have them brought up to speed in no time.''

Stephen nodded.

''Do you want me to stay for the meeting with Fieldman's?''

''No need.'' It was Stephen's turn to grin. ''I canceled it yesterday.''

''Of course you did.''

Lyle was chuckling as he walked out the door. When Stephen closed it behind the man and turned to face Catherine she swore the room got smaller.

''You didn't have to come.''

It didn't sound like a criticism, but the intense way in which he watched her made her uneasy, defensive.

''I felt I did.''

''Satisfied with the payback?''

''That's not why I'm here.''

''No?'' He'd walked forward as they spoke, and now he stood near enough that she was forced to look up, despite the stylish Italian pumps that added nearly three inches to her height.

''I thought you might need me.''

Something flickered briefly in his eyes and one side of his mouth lifted. ''Worried about me?''

''I hear that's what wives do,'' she said lightly.

She thought of the other things wives did and nearly blushed. Just for a moment she was tempted to reach out, trail a fingertip over his chest and then use his very tasteful silk tie to pull him forward for a kiss. God, the man wore clothes well, which made her curious about what lay beneath them. They could lock the door, request that his secretary hold all calls. A vivid picture of what could come next filled her mind, shocking in all its sensuous detail.

She blinked and took a step back. What was wrong with her? She'd never entertained thoughts like this before. Indeed, she hadn't thought herself capable of sexual fantasies. But this one was a doozy, not to mention highly impractical. After all, a desktop *had* to be incredibly uncomfortable.

She was sleep-deprived; that was it. And there was no denying that Stephen was an attractive man. Stress. She filed the excuses away, satisfied that at least her brain still seemed capable of functioning. She'd wondered for a moment there.

''Everything okay?'' he asked.

''Fine. I'd better be going.''

''Busy day today?'' He said it without the sneer that she now realized Derek had often used when referring to her work.

''Yes, I have a meeting at noon to discuss Project Christmas.''

"Project Christmas? It's August."

"The end of August. And Danbury's has had wool sweaters on display for at least a month."

"Touché."

"Planning takes time if you want to do something right. I don't believe in doing things halfway."

She watched one dark eyebrow lift, but he said nothing. And again she thought about his desk and the sizzling fantasy that her sleep-deprived, stressed-out brain had manufactured. Catherine was not a woman known for her spontaneity, and yet she wondered if planning were required to do something like *that* right.

She had to clear her throat before she could reply. "We can count on Danbury's to host our drop boxes again this year, I hope?"

"Of course. Project Christmas is a great cause."

She nodded in agreement, grateful for the return of a steady heartbeat. "No child should have to go without gifts at Christmas, which is why I know Danbury's will also be generous with its corporate donation."

He smiled. "You're very smooth. I almost didn't feel you pick my pocket."

"Thanks." She pulled the thin strap of her purse over her shoulder. "Well, I should go."

"Yes."

They stood facing each other for an awkward moment.

"The move going okay?"

"Yes, fine."

She'd spent the better part of the previous evening unpacking the boxes the movers had brought, which had given her the perfect excuse to stay in her bedroom for the remainder of the night. Not that it had mattered. He'd left shortly before six and had not returned by the time she'd called it a night at ten o'clock. Where had he gone? For the first time she'd wondered if Stephen had a girlfriend. Rosaria had said Catherine wasn't his usual type. What or *who* was?

She found herself in an odd sort of conundrum. She didn't want to spend time alone with Stephen, and yet she liked even less the idea that he might be spending his time with someone else.

"I'm going to see my parents tonight. I have to tell them before a reporter calls for comment. I thought, if your schedule is clear, we could go over there this evening. That's if you want to go with me."

"I wouldn't expect you to go alone." He tucked his hands into the front pockets of his dark gray trousers and tilted his head to one side, looking oddly nervous. "How do you think they'll take it?"

You're a Danbury, she almost said. One Danbury would be as good as another to her mother. The connections, the social position, the prestige…the money.

"They'll be a little surprised." She offered a small smile.

He didn't smile. "I'll bet."

"What time do you think you'll be home?"

"Six."

And she would be there, she realized, in his big, quiet home, waiting for him.

"We'll just drop by my parents' house for drinks. I won't make you sit through an entire meal, I promise."

He walked her to the door of his office, opened it and then stood there for a moment, leaning against the jamb. "I wouldn't mind. They're bound to have questions."

Yes, Catherine thought. But she didn't have answers. At least not ones they would like hearing.

"Drinks only."

"Will you tell them about the codicil?" he asked. "No."

"I didn't think so, but I just thought we should have our stories straight."

As she boarded the elevator, and hit the button marked "lobby", it saddened Catherine to realize that her parents would understand marriage as a business arrangement. After all, it was what they had. It was why they had thought her foolish for not marrying Derek even after his duplicity had been exposed. And not for the first time she wondered if the cool reserve for which she'd become well known was a byproduct of her parents' cold union.

Stephen was not home when Catherine arrived at his house late that afternoon, but the movers had dropped off another batch of boxes. Last night she had been grateful to immerse herself in the tedious chore of unpacking and assigning other boxes to storage in Stephen's attic. Now she was simply too tired to hunt through the boxes for the shoes she wanted to wear that evening.

Her cell phone rang as she contemplated where to start. She pulled it from her purse and sank onto her bed, grateful for the reprieve.

"Hello?"

"Cath, it's Felicity. Where are you?"

"I'm…home," she said, not quite ready to explain. She'd rather get it all over in one shot, which was why she'd asked Felicity, who still lived with their parents, to be sure to be there that evening.

"You're not home. I dropped by your apartment to borrow your diamond choker and the doorman said you had moved out. What's going on?"

Catherine sighed. "I'll explain tonight at the house. It's really not something I want to discuss over the phone."

"Are you in trouble?"

"Of course not."

She was touched by her self-centered little sister's concern until Felicity added, "That's a relief. You've already upset everyone enough by calling off the wedding. And then we've had to endure the tabloid stories. Mother's so embarrassed she hasn't been to the club in weeks, and I can hardly go out of the house without being laughed at."

"Yes, I know what a trial this has been for her, and for all of you," she said, somehow managing to keep sarcasm out of her voice. Just once, she thought, it would be nice to have someone in her family worry about her feelings and be supportive of her decisions. Perhaps she would get her wish later that night. "I've got to go. I'll see you around eight."

She hung up, even less enthusiastic about spending the next couple of hours unpacking than she had been before, so she decided to stall a little longer.

In the kitchen, she took a glass from the cupboard and went to the fridge for some orange juice. She noticed the cake right away. It was a double-layer with chocolate frosting. Not quite half of it was missing. Stephen's birthday cake. Much as it should have pleased her that he had had someone with whom he could celebrate, she couldn't suppress the spurt of jealousy that that someone had not been her.

Catherine chose a beige linen pantsuit to wear to her parents' house. Her mother would frown on the pants. Her mother often frowned, though, making pleasing her a virtual impossibility. Besides, Catherine figured by the time Deirdra Canton heard the word "married", she wouldn't be paying any mind to her daughter's wardrobe. She heard Stephen coming up the stairs as she put on her earrings. Sticking her head out the door, she watched him jog up the last few steps and turn in the opposite direction.

"Hello."

He turned, startled. "Hi."

She was surprised, too. The neat executive was nowhere to be found. In his place stood a sweaty man in gray cotton shorts and a T-shirt, hair windblown and skin glowing from exertion.

"You're ready."

She raised an eyebrow. "You're not."

"I heard the water running in your room when I got home. I figured I had time for a run and quick shower before you were ready. Most women…" He wisely let the thought go unfinished. "Give me fifteen minutes," he said.

She allowed her gaze to roam over the damp T-shirt that seemed molded to his powerful build. The fantasy she'd entertained in his office that morning came back to her in a breath-stealing rush. "Take twenty."

Catherine used the extra time to do some more unpacking, figuring the monotony would keep her mind off inappropriate thoughts. She had finally managed to reel in her pulse when, arms loaded with lingerie, she turned to find Stephen standing in her open doorway. His dark gaze lingered on the silky garments she clutched in her hands.

"I wondered…"

"Wondered what?" she asked, as she hastily stuffed the assorted unmentionables into the top drawer of the bureau without bothering to neatly fold and arrange them.

"I wondered…if this was appropriate attire for meeting the in-laws."

He wore a lightweight sport coat, crisp white shirt

and dark trousers. He'd forgone a tie, a definite no-no in her mother's book.

"Perfect."

The Cantons were already having drinks when Stephen and Catherine arrived. The economic downturn had decimated Deirdra and Russell Canton's once robust stock portfolio, but it had not changed the way they lived. They still insisted on having the best of everything, because keeping up appearances was more important than the fact their retirement funds were nearly gone, their savings obliterated and the house had been remortgaged twice.

Her parents and sister were seated in the room her mother insisted on calling the front parlor. They had no back parlor, so Catherine's practical mind had never understood the need for the distinction. As long as she could remember the room had been decorated the same, with spindly-legged antique chairs and a settee that had once belonged to her mother's mother. It was indeed a parlor, Catherine had thought more than once: a funeral parlor.

"Someday the furniture will be yours," Deirdra Canton had said often enough. Catherine considered the words a vague kind of threat, as if someday her own personality would be stamped out of existence and she would become her mother.

Not that she didn't love her mother, she just didn't believe they had much in common—whether it was their taste in furniture or their support for social causes for that matter. Deirdra Canton sat on beautification committees and raised funds for animal shelters. Worthy causes, certainly, but Catherine thought it more important to wade into the trenches to reach people who were too frightened and desperate to notice the lilies blooming in a downtown garden and too poor to afford food for their children, let alone their pets.

Her parents had objected to her having a career until she'd snagged a position at the shelter. It was close enough to charity work in their book so as not to raise eyebrows among their friends, whose debutante daughters had ensured their social standing by marrying well soon after college. Apparently her parents had entertained the same notion, expecting Catherine to earn a degree but not actually use it. Just as they had provided the scholarship that had allowed a young girl from one of Chicago's roughest neighborhoods to attend the same exclusive prep school Catherine had. Then they had objected strenuously when the girl had become Catherine's friend.

"We don't become involved with people like that on a personal level," her mother had chastised her more than once.

Catherine was still haunted by that lack of involvement, and what had happened to the young girl who, despite Deirdra's objections, had become Catherine's most treasured friend.

"Are you going to stand there staring at the furniture, dear?'' her mother asked with an embarrassed laugh.

"Sorry, my mind was elsewhere. Mother, Dad, Felicity—you remember Stephen Danbury?''

Her father stood, shook Stephen's hand. Her mother remained seated, smiling politely. Felicity offered a feline grin. At eighteen she had mastered flirtation. Indeed, she could have given Catherine lessons.

"It's nice to see you all again.''

"We didn't realize when you said you would be bringing someone that it would be Stephen. How is your cousin?'' Deirdra asked.

The inquiry was her mother's polite way of being rude.

"I'd imagine he has worked his way to irate right about now," Stephen said. Reaching for Catherine's hand, he added, "Catherine and I have some news.''

"News?'' her mother and father asked in unison.

Felicity, glancing at their linked fingers, muttered, "I have a feeling this is going to be bad.''

"We're…married," Catherine said, deciding to just get it all out there at once. This discussion wasn't the sort that one could ease into anyway.

"M-married?'' Deirdra sputtered, her face a study in surprise, and not the good kind. What little hope Catherine had held that her parents would be pleased enough with her new status to overlook her serious breach in family etiquette faded away.

"When did this happen?'' her father asked.

"We were married over the weekend, sir," Stephen replied. "It was all very spur-of-the-moment."

"I'll say." Russell tossed back the last of his Scotch and scowled.

"But where?" Deirdra asked, as some of the color returned to her cheeks.

"In Las Vegas," Stephen said, and Catherine watched the color leak out again. In fact her mother's eyelids flickered delicately, as if she might faint dead away. At another time her mother's flair for drama might have been comical. But there was nothing funny about the tension snapping like an exposed electrical wire in the Cantons' staid front parlor.

"Great! Just great!" Felicity stormed. "The tabloids were just starting to forget about us. I leave for college in a week, Cath. One week! How could you do this to me?"

"I didn't do anything to you," Catherine said. "In fact, given the way the press has hovered since… Well, we just wanted something simple and private."

"And tacky, too, apparently," Deirdra harrumphed. Her near fainting spell had apparently passed.

"We wanted you all to be there, of course," Catherine said, as if her mother hadn't spoken. "It just seemed better this way."

"Well, then, by all means, let's pop out the bubbly," Felicity snarled. "We still have a few cases left over from Cath's other wedding, don't we, Daddy?"

"Felicity, there's no need for your editorial comment," Russell said.

"Yes, stop your annoying chatter," Deirdra added. "You're giving me one of my migraines."

Felicity sat down on the settee, outwardly subdued. This was quite the role reversal, Catherine thought. Usually Catherine toed the line that Felicity regularly stepped over. Catherine hadn't merely strayed a few inches into forbidden territory, though. With her unexpected marriage to Stephen she had taken one huge flying leap.

"I can't believe you did this," her mother said.

"We're very disappointed," her father added.

"I apologize for not including all of you in our plans or the ceremony," Stephen said. "Catherine wanted to, but I insisted on secrecy. I felt it would be best to do this quickly and quietly."

As he accepted the blame, he tucked her hand into the crook of his arm. The gesture seemed both chivalrous and protective. It seemed to say, *We are a unit.* And so it gave her strength.

Deirdra waved away his explanation. "There's going to be plenty of talk now. Is *this*—" she said the word "this" as if it referred to something vile "—why things didn't work out with Derek?"

"This has nothing to do with Derek," Catherine replied, and then felt her face heat. In a way, it had *everything* to do with Derek.

"What were you thinking, Catherine?" her father asked.

Anger rose to the surface, the source of which she could not determine. But it was there, bubbling hot, as impossible to hold back as steam from a boiling pot. "I was thinking you'd be happy for me. I was thinking that after the fiasco with Derek you might be wish me well."

"But *Stephen*?" Her mother sighed, as if the man were not standing in the room.

Beside her, Catherine felt him stiffen. "What's the problem, Mother? He's a good man, and I know it can't be his pedigree. He comes from the same family as Derek."

"But…" Deirdra let the thought go unfinished.

"But what?" Catherine persisted.

"I think I know where this is heading," Stephen said, his voice quiet, his features tight. "I'm not the right Danbury, am I, Mrs. Canton?"

"It's nothing like that."

"Like what? What's going on here?" Catherine asked, but she was afraid she knew. And it horrified her to think that her own mother could harbor the kind of prejudices that had already so wounded the man standing beside her.

"We're sure you're a fine man, Stephen. We just don't know you well," her father said.

"You can get to know him." You can get to know both of us, she almost said, because in that instant she realized there was more than one stranger in the room.

Perhaps it was her pleading stare, or the fact that her mother preferred entertaining to arguing, but her parents seemed to thaw a little. Resignation,

Catherine decided, would be a welcome substitute for acceptance at this point.

"I'd love some champagne," Deirdra said. "Fetch a bottle from the cellar, would you, Russell? Felicity can get the glasses."

She waved Catherine and Stephen toward the settee. "Come and sit."

Catherine had barely settled onto the brocade upholstery when her mother added, "One day, you know, that settee will be yours."

CHAPTER SIX

"THAT went well," Catherine said as they drove home after one of the most excruciatingly long and awkward hours of her life.

"Yeah. I'm sure they won't go into mourning when our marriage ends."

"Sorry about that."

"We are what we are, Catherine." And she knew he was talking about more than her parents.

Neither one spoke again until they arrived at the house. He parked the car in the garage and then held the back door for her.

As they passed through the kitchen, Catherine said, "Are you hungry?"

"Starving."

The way he looked at her when he said it had her mouth going dry. Something simmered in his dark eyes, and the memory of their last kiss stirred her blood.

"I could fix you a sandwich."

"A sandwich?" He smiled as if she'd told a joke. "Why not? But I'll fix it myself. Is there anything you want?"

His question went beyond cold cuts, she was sure.

She shook her head. "I'll keep you company, if you'd like?"

"I'd like."

She sat in the nook and watched him, the wealthy head of one of the most recognizable store chains in America, move around in the well-planned room in his stockinged feet.

When he was seated across from her, a huge sandwich and generous wedge of cake filling his plate, she said, "It looks like someone remembered your birthday."

"Rosaria made it."

Relief had her grinning. "I met her the other day."

"Yes. She mentioned it."

"She seems very nice. Does she just work for you the one day a week?"

Sandwich half way to his mouth, he paused. "Excuse me."

"She mentioned that she does the grocery shopping for you."

He dumped the sandwich back onto the plate. His tone angry, glacial, he said, "And you want to know what days she works for me?"

"I believe that's what I asked."

"Because someone who looks like her would of course be the hired help?"

"Stephen, did I miss something here? You're suddenly angry and I have no idea why."

"Of course you don't. I don't know why I expected

you to. We are what we are,'' he said, echoing his words from the drive home.

"If I've said something to offend you, please tell me so I can apologize."

"Drop it. It's not important."

"It seems important to you. I'd like to know—"

"Rosaria is my aunt," he interrupted. "You assumed she was the hired help."

It was her turn to be angry. "Yes, I assumed. I saw a woman, wearing a uniform, putting away groceries in your kitchen. I put two and two together and came up with four."

"Because that's the stereotype."

"Because no one told me differently."

"And it never occurred to you that I would have family?" His voice rose and he said something in Spanish that she decided was not at all pleasant. "I do. A family that looks a hell of a lot more like me than I look like the Danburys. It is because of them that I know how to speak my mother's language, even though my grandparents forbade me from doing so in their home. That only made me all the more determined to become fluent, which I was by the time I was thirteen."

"Did you see them regularly, then?"

"I saw my maternal grandmother every day. When the Danburys wouldn't allow her to visit me she offered to clean their house. She hired in as their maid so that she could be near me."

His voice shook with emotion—anger, and something else that caused Catherine's heart to ache for the little boy who had been denied so much.

"It's because of *mi abuelita* that I have pictures of my mother. My grandparents would not allow a single snapshot of her to be displayed. They were ashamed of her, ashamed that their Harvard-educated son had married a Puerto Rican maid who spoke broken English."

"Oh, Stephen. I'm sorry. I didn't know." She reached across the table to touch his hand. But he pulled away.

"Now you do."

The silence stretched, before she asked in a quiet voice, "Do they know about me? I know Rosaria does, but do the others?"

"I've told them about our arrangement, yes."

"Oh." He'd told them about their *arrangement*. She could only wonder what they must think of her.

"Will I meet them?"

"No. I see no point in that. You talk a good game when it comes to acceptance and equality, but the first time you run across a brown-skinned woman in a kitchen you automatically assume she's there because someone has paid her to tidy up. You disappoint me, Catherine. I didn't think you were so much like your mother."

Stephen said the words, and in his anger he meant the words, but then he watched her face pale and he wished he could snatch them back.

She scooted off the bench seat, eyes overly bright.

Her voice was a shaky whisper when she said, "I'm sorry."

And then she was gone.

Stephen's appetite fled as well, taking with it all his anger. Now he just felt like a heel. Catherine had had a stressful and not entirely pleasant day, and he'd just made it worse. He tossed his uneaten sandwich down the garbage disposal, along with the cake, and turned off the kitchen light. The house was quiet, and even though for the first time since he'd bought it six years earlier someone else was sharing it with him, it still felt empty.

And he still felt alone.

The rest of the week passed much as Stephen had expected it would. He and Catherine rarely saw one another, and yet they each managed to evade or else lie convincingly to the handful of persistent tabloid reporters who dogged their steps, hoping for confirmation of rumors of a Vegas wedding. An Oscar-winning star's brush with the law thinned the ranks of the vultures, but the speculation continued. *Celebrity Spyglass* featured the couple inside, along with a reprint of the photograph that had been taken of them aboard his sailboat in July and then been run prominently in the tabloid the following week, with the headline: *Is this why the wedding is off?* This time the headline asked, *Are they or aren't they?*

Even he wasn't sure he had an answer to that one.

At home each night, the only evidence that Stephen

shared his house with someone else was a small sliver of light from beneath Catherine's tightly closed bedroom door. She closeted herself inside before he arrived home and, to his surprise, was gone each morning before he left at seven.

Saturday morning, however, she was seated in the breakfast nook, enjoying a cup of coffee, when he walked into the room. An empty bowl sat on the table and she was reading the newspaper. Two things struck him immediately. She wasn't wearing any makeup and she was dressed in pajamas. She didn't need eyeliner and blusher to make her lovely. Those blue eyes needed no enhancing and neither did those high cheekbones. As for her clothing, he decided she could wear burlap and belt it with twine and still look classy enough to have tea with the Queen.

They had hardly spoken since the last time they'd been together in the kitchen, and his conscience nipped him hard. He owed her an apology.

"Good morning," she said.

"Good morning."

"I made coffee."

"Smells good."

"And tastes all right, too," she said, taking a sip. "I'm done with the paper." She folded up the *Tribune* and scooted it to the other side of the table.

He couldn't stand another minute of this polite, trite conversation.

"About Tuesday night. I'm sorry. I didn't mean to bite your head off."

"It's forgotten." She waved one delicate-looking hand. The cheap band on her ring finger somehow managed to catch and reflect the light. He'd have to do something about that, he decided.

He helped himself to some coffee and sat across from her. Something was on her mind. He could tell by the way she shifted in her seat. She didn't fidget, precisely. Someone who looked like Catherine didn't fidget. But she was ill at ease, apprehensive.

"What is it?"

"Excuse me?"

"Something's on your mind."

"I have a…function tonight. A ball and silent auction to raise funds for literacy. I didn't organize it, but the committee is hoping that I…that *we* will be there. If you're not free, I'll understand. It is rather short notice."

"Black tie?"

"Yes."

"What time?"

"Six."

"I'll be happy to escort you."

"We'll be the center of attention," she said, her tone apologetic. "They'll all be wondering about our marriage."

Stephen had long been the subject of gossip. This would be nothing new. But he meant it when he said, "Then we'll be sure to give them something good to talk about."

That evening, as he stood in his foyer and watched

Catherine walk down the stairs, he knew they would indeed be the talk of the town. His beautiful Ice Princess wore fiery red, an off-the shoulder sheath of curve-hugging material that reached to her ankles and shimmered with each step she took. She wore heels, the strappy kind that showed off neatly painted toenails the same color as her dress, and she'd left her hair loose.

"Encantador," he murmured.

"What does it mean?"

"Lovely."

"Thank you. And you look handsome. How would I say that?"

"Guapo."

"Muy guapo," she said, with a lift of her brows, adding the Spanish word for "very." Full lips bowed into a smile that was as red and tempting as her dress.

The ballroom at the Sheraton Towers was already jammed with several hundred of Chicago's wealthiest and most influential people when they arrived. Stephen recognized many people in the crowd. Some had even been frequent guests at his grandparents' home while Stephen was growing up. But he didn't consider any of them his friends, and the feeling was mutual. He nodded politely, as did they, and offered the standard greetings.

Catherine, however, worked the room like a veteran politician, shaking hands, air-kissing cheeks, chuckling in that reserved way of hers at every joke or even mildly humorous remark. He'd never seen this side of her at other social functions, but he should have guessed it was there. It was what made her such a good fund-raiser. She knew much of society thought her a vapid and wealthy woman who merely played at her job with the shelter, and she was smart enough to use it to her advantage, coaxing dollars from their pockets in much the same way a snake charmer coaxes a cobra from its basket.

The seating was assigned—each round, linen-covered table set with service for ten. No one was at Catherine and Stephen's table yet except for an older couple, Enid and Oscar Dersham. Stephen recognized them as contemporaries of his grandparents, although he didn't recall them coming to the house often, maybe just at Christmas for the annual party.

He snagged two glasses of champagne and headed in the direction of the table, content to wait there for Catherine. But he was waylaid before he could get there by a woman he had dated casually the summer before.

"I've heard a nasty rumor," Cherise Langston said.

She stood much too close to him as she spoke, and had the audacity to take one of the flutes of champagne he held and sip from it. Her forward behavior was just one of the reasons he'd broken things off with her long before they could become serious.

"Hello, Cherise."

"You're looking as tasty as ever, Stephen. So, is it true?"

He decided to play dumb. "True?"

"The rumor about you and Catherine Canton. The tabloids are claiming the two of you are married."

"Catherine is my wife," he said succinctly.

Her eyes widened, filled with malice, although her tone managed to stay light. "And you told me you weren't the marrying kind. I believe your exact words were, 'I don't plan to make that kind of commitment to anyone.'"

He had said that, and he'd meant it, but that had been long before he'd learned about the codicil. Long before Catherine.

"I changed my mind."

"Are you trying to tell me you fell in love with Catherine Canton?" She laughed, a grating noise that he'd found annoying even when he'd also found her attractive. Now it was truly offensive.

"I found it hard to believe when she snagged your cousin, but then Derek likes a challenge, and he's unencumbered by a conscience. I hear he was putting the moves on the wedding planner just minutes before their ceremony."

When he didn't dignify her speculation with a response, she continued. "What a waste of manhood." She held out her glass and clinked it against his in a toast. "Call me when you need some warming up. I'm not partial to playing second fiddle, but for you I'll make an exception. *Hasta luego*, sweetheart."

Catherine joined him at their table a few minutes later, already looking tired, though she camouflaged it well enough. She greeted the Dershams with her usual charm.

"You're looking well. Have you met my husband yet?"

"Your husband?" Enid Dersham glanced around the room. "We thought the wedding had been... No, dear, where is he?"

Catherine's laughter was mild and musical, taking the sting out of the awkward situation.

"He's right here. Stephen Danbury, may I present Mr. and Mrs. Dersham?" To Stephen, she said, "The Dershams have been incredibly generous to several children's charities, as well as avid supporters of the arts."

The Dershams eyed Stephen, clearly puzzled, but too polite to say so.

"We knew Stephen's grandparents. Very nice people," Enid said.

"Yes," Oscar chimed in, and, directing his comments to Stephen, added, "Your grandparents are sorely missed. They were true pillars of the community."

"Our grandparents were something," Derek said, causing all heads to turn in his direction. He stood just behind Catherine, bitterness making his eyes overly bright. "Catherine, you're looking well for someone who just stomped on my heart."

She didn't buy his words for a minute. His ego might have been bruised, but his heart had never been at risk.

"This is a surprise. I don't believe I ever had much success in talking you into coming to these functions."

She knew he considered it easier to write a check than to suffer through an evening of small talk.

"I'm only too happy to support a good cause," he replied smoothly, smiling for the Dershams' benefit. To Enid, he said in a stage whisper, "She broke my heart by marrying my cousin, you know, but life goes on."

"Office cleaned out yet?" Stephen asked. He draped an arm over the back of Catherine's chair, the move casual and yet proprietary.

Derek pretended not to hear him, but the tic in his cheek gave away his irritation. "All's fair in love and business. I came over here hoping to bury the hatchet."

Stephen snorted out a laugh. "Yes, which is why I'll be sure not to turn my back on you this evening."

People were starting to stare, as well as straining their ears to listen. No doubt word had already gotten around the massive ballroom that both Danbury heirs were present and a confrontation was ensuing. Catherine nearly groaned. As if there wasn't enough for the gossips to speculate on and twitter over. There would be no silencing the busybodies, but at least she could ensure the cousins were kept separate.

"Let's dance," she said, rising from her seat and forcing Stephen to stop glowering at Derek. "I love this song," she added, before realizing that the number the band was presently playing was the old Nat King Cole favorite "When I Fall in Love."

She took his hand and led him to the dance floor. The song was just ending as they turned to face one another.

Silvia Rathburn, one of the organizers of the event, rushed toward the stage.

"Don't go anywhere," she said as she passed Catherine and Stephen.

Silvia was a plump woman who considered pink her trademark color. She was wearing a shade just this side of shocking, and a gown whose cut was more suited to a prom-goer than a woman approaching her sixties. Catherine had worked with the woman on several projects, though, and knew her heart was far more generous than her fashion sense. At the microphone, the woman clapped her hands together as if to gain everyone's attention.

"I want to remind everyone that bidding on the silent auction will continue until we are seated for dinner. And I have an announcement to make. Would you all raise your glasses in a toast? It seems we have something else to celebrate this evening."

Catherine felt her mouth go dry as the woman winked at her, and she felt Stephen's arm tighten around her waist, as if he too were bracing himself for the inevitable.

"I know none of us likes to admit we read the tabloids, but sometimes, amid the stories of alien abductions and forty-five-pound newborns, they get things right. A little birdie just told me that Catherine Canton and Derek—'' She blushed, as embarrassed as they were by the unfortunate *faux pas*. ''Excuse me. My apologies. That is, Catherine and *Stephen* Danbury exchanged vows last weekend. Please join me in wishing the newlyweds every happiness.''

The noise level in the room immediately rose, along with the champagne glasses. Catherine and Stephen stood alone in the middle of the large dance floor, truly the center of attention.

''Well, I'd say our secret is out,'' Stephen said in a quiet voice. ''Are you okay?''

''They'd all have found out eventually,'' Catherine replied, somehow managing to keep a pleasant little smile curving her lips. The dimple winked and he admired her aplomb. And, though he rarely speculated about what others thought, he couldn't help wondering what was crossing the minds of this roomful of Chicago's elite.

The men would be jealous, he decided, looking at the lovely woman in his arms. The women? Envious that they didn't have Catherine's beauty or grace.

From the stage, Silvia continued, ''The tabloids say they got married in Las Vegas, so I'm sure they didn't have an opportunity to share a dance. I thought they could do that now.''

She motioned for the orchestra to begin playing, and the first strains of ''As Time Goes By'' filled the room.

Stephen couldn't resist teasing her with a famous

line from the movie that had made that song famous. "Here's looking at you, kid."

He took her hand in his, raised it to his mouth and kissed the back of it. The women in the room sighed in unison, and Stephen told himself it had been entirely for show. She looked so lovely, a cross between Ingrid Bergman and Grace Kelly with her classical features and aloof mannerisms. As he rested his other hand on her slender waist he was suddenly grateful his grandmother had insisted on all those dance lessons he'd once considered a waste of time.

He led and she followed. She rested her cheek against his jaw and he tightened his hand around her waist, pulling her closer. Pulling them both in. The music stopped, but he didn't release her.

"You dance beautifully," she said.

"Three years of lessons, courtesy of my grandmother."

"God bless her."

He laughed softly. "I cursed her at the time, but I was just thinking the same thing."

She glanced around. "The music has stopped."

"So it has." He lowered his head.

"W-what are you doing?" she whispered.

"Satisfying their curiosity."

He'd said something similar that day in his bedroom. But that kiss hadn't been so much satisfying as disturbing. The same thing, he realized, could be said about this one. Need speared through him, welcome and intrusive at the same time, taking as much as it gave in return. Mere attraction? He wanted to think so. That would be so much tidier and more simple than anything else. But something nagged at him.

He mulled it over for the rest of the evening. Studied it, and Catherine, as he would any vexing problem found within Danbury's books. After all, at its core that was what this was: a business arrangement. And yet he could not honestly say his heart had ever pounded like a jackhammer when going over fourth-quarter earnings or market share data.

It was nearly midnight before they had inched their way toward the exits.

"I'll get your wrap," Stephen offered. "Why don't you say goodbye to whomever you need to say goodbye to, and I'll meet you by the coat check?"

Catherine smiled. "You read my mind. Give me ten minutes, and if I'm not there, send out a search party."

He was barely out of earshot when Derek sidled up next to her.

"Quite the cozy portrait of marital bliss you two painted tonight."

"Goodnight, Derek."

She turned to leave, but he grabbed her by the elbow. His grip was firm enough that extracting herself would have caused a scene. He, of course, knew this.

"What do you want?"

"Just wanted to wish you luck."

"Why would I require luck?"

"This is a game, isn't it?"

She didn't respond.

"A high-stakes game," he added. "Even a do-gooder of your caliber is in over her head, Catherine."

"I don't know what you're talking about. Now, please release me."

"Catherine, Catherine. He's using you."

"You would know all about that, wouldn't you?"

"Stephen likes to play chess."

His *non sequitur* threw her. "What?"

"You know—chess. The game where the object is to capture the other player's queen. You have to think carefully before each move. In fact, you have to think several moves ahead. It's about strategy."

"I'm familiar with the game."

"Ask yourself this: why did you come to the choir loft?"

"I received a note. And a good thing, I'd say."

"Who sent the note?"

She shrugged. "I thought it was you, but obviously not. Whoever sent it, I owe him or her a debt of gratitude."

"I'd say you're already paying it."

"Are you implying Stephen sent me the note?"

"Ah, now you're catching on. He set me up, Catherine. He knew about the will's codicil and he had to make sure I didn't get married."

"Even if that's the case, did you have to fall so neatly into his trap?"

"How do you know he didn't bribe the wedding planner to seduce me?"

"Because if you'd truly loved me you wouldn't have been seduced."

"Do you think Stephen loves you?"

She didn't answer. This wasn't about love.

"Just watch your back. He's using you." And with that he was gone, leaving unsettling questions in his wake.

Stephen walked Catherine to her door. Her bedroom door. It seemed silly and unnecessary and sweet all at once. Something fluttered insider her. Anticipation? Nerves?

Suspicion?

Derek's words echoed in her head. She pushed them aside, but her hammering heart was not so easily ignored.

"I had a good time tonight," he said.

"You sound surprised."

"Those things usually aren't very entertaining."

"Must have been the company," she replied.

His smile came slowly. "Must have been."

No one was present to fool, but he sounded so sincere. Suddenly she needed to know.

"Did you send me the note?"

"Note?"

"On my wedding day. At the church. Did you send me the note to meet Derek in the loft?"

His eyebrows lifted in…surprise? Dismay? But his voice held neither when he replied, "I did."

Her heart twisted. "Why?"

He ran a hand through his hair, nearly turned away. But then he leveled that intense gaze at her instead. "I thought you should know. It wasn't the first time I'd seen Derek with someone else. While you were dating there were…others."

"Others?" Now it was her stomach that felt knotted. "But why didn't you tell me then, or after Derek proposed? Why did you wait until my wedding day?"

His gaze remained intense, but some other indecipherable emotion seemed to cloud his dark eyes. "It wasn't any of my business. But you seemed nice and, well, I overheard him tell the wedding planner to meet him in the loft. I thought you could assess the situation for yourself, make your own decision."

It seemed to make sense, not quite chivalrous, but close, and in keeping with Stephen's aloof nature. Still, doubts nibbled at her.

"You didn't know about the codicil then, though? Right?"

"Why the sudden questions?"

"I'm wondering, that's all."

"That's not all. You could have asked these questions at any time. Why now? Did Derek say something to you tonight that has you suspicious of my motives?"

"No, nothing." She waved a hand, hoping to dispel the tension that had crept between them. Derek's doing, she realized, and hated herself for handing him so easy a victory.

"He must have said something."

"He just mentioned the note and said he thought you'd sent it. He said… It doesn't matter."

"Clearly it does."

He seemed irritated and cold once again, not at all the man who had danced with her in the ballroom and stolen her breath with a kiss.

"He just made sure to remind me that you had a lot to gain if he didn't get married that day."

"Yeah, well, I didn't know that, but he did. And he's right. I had a lot to gain. I had even more to gain when I married you. You knew that, and yet you still proposed. Remember that, Catherine. You popped the question, not me."

"Yes. I'm sorry. Let's forget about this. It doesn't matter. Derek is only trying to make trouble."

He shook his head, resignation edging his tone when he said, "I thought you would have figured it out by now. That's Derek's specialty. Goodnight, Catherine."

He turned away before she could say another word. At the other end of the long hallway she heard his bedroom door snap shut. With a heavy heart, she closed her own.

CHAPTER SEVEN

GIVEN his growing attraction to her, Stephen found living with Catherine a test of his will-power. Still, he rather enjoyed discovering her quirky habits and surprising interests. She was a good cook, better than he'd imagined a woman who grew up in a household where there was a hired professional to prepare the meals would be. He'd bet his last buck her mother didn't know how to boil water and had not encouraged Catherine's interest in the culinary arts.

And while she cooked she liked to sing. He found it amazing that a woman who looked like Catherine could be so tone deaf. He was surprised his Lab didn't start howling whenever she tried to hit a high note. Of course, the dog wasn't willing to bite that hand that fed him. And Catherine did a whole lot more than feed Degas. She'd barely been in the house a week when Stephen discovered his fickle hound camped outside her door. Now Degas was sharing her bed.

Lucky dog.

Stephen and Catherine had found some surprising common ground: old movies. He had long been a fan of black and white flicks. The genre didn't matter, although he was partial to Alfred Hitchcock and anything that starred Humphrey Bogart. They had that in common, except for her it was Cary Grant. She could recite entire scenes from *An Affair to Remember*. For him, it was *Rear Window* and *The Maltese Falcon*.

A few times a week they would spend a couple of hours in one another's company, suitably chaperoned by the work of some legendary Hollywood filmmaker. Then they would walk up the stairs together as the house grew dark and quiet around them, offer one another a stilted goodnight and turn their separate ways. Long afterward he'd lie awake on the cool sheets of his big bed, wondering if the same need that hummed through his blood was depriving her of sleep as well.

Most weekends they spent following their own pursuits. This weekend, however, they were expected at a tribute dinner Saturday night that the fire department was putting on to raise funds for the families of three firefighters who had died battling a warehouse blaze earlier in the year. The invitation had come to the house, addressed to the both of them, marking the first time they were invited to an event as Mr. and Mrs. Stephen Danbury. Stephen didn't really want to go. The gossip and speculation about their marriage had yet to quiet down. But he was just old-fashioned enough to believe that where his wife went he went, despite the particulars of their marriage.

Catherine plucked the square of ivory vellum off her bureau and tucked it into the small beaded clutch that was the same shade of emerald as the full-length gown she wore. The gown was new, a flirty Versace that left one shoulder bare and required her to skimp on dinner to wear it to its best possible advantage.

She was checking her reflection in the mirror a second time when Stephen tapped on her door.

"Catherine, we're already fashionably late," he called.

Even so, she reapplied her lipstick and fussed with her hair, which she'd left loose again, before opening the door, and was satisfied to see him suck in a breath.

"You do Versace proud," Stephen said. He took her by the hand, forcing her to turn a full three-hundred-and-sixty degrees.

"Thank you. And Armani looks good on you." She adjusted his bow tie, which was perfectly knotted, and used their close proximity as an excuse to brush non-existent lint from the lapels of his tuxedo jacket. "Have I ever told you that you wear clothes well?"

She was flirting, but she couldn't resist. He looked so handsome, so…interested.

"I can't say that you have." He leaned in, bringing with him the crisp scents of soap and aftershave. "Let's make this an early night."

She held her breath and tried not think about the double entendre when she replied, "Oh, is there something you want to do?"

Dark eyes seemed to smolder.

"As a matter of fact, there is."

The evening dragged, perhaps because the enigmatic answer Stephen had given before they left the house lingered in her mind, tantalizing her with its possible interpretations. It didn't help that as they ate, danced, or shared small talk with acquaintances she would look up to find him studying her in that intense way of his. She was in the middle of a conversation with the Mayor, pitching hard for more funds for youth activities, when he joined her.

"Ah, Stephen, I was just enjoying a conversation with your lovely wife," the Mayor said, offering a hand.

The two men shook, and it was obvious this was not a first meeting.

"Has she muscled some more money out of you yet?" he asked. There was pride in his voice, warmth in his smile, and heat in the hand he rested on the small of her back.

"The city's budget being what it is, not quite. But she's very persuasive."

"She is that. I'm afraid I'm going to have to steal her away now. We have another engagement."

She glanced at him in surprise and resisted the urge to ask what that engagement was.

"Of course. I understand. Newlyweds have all sorts of *engagements*," the Mayor remarked with a wink.

Stephen hustled Catherine out the door in record time, tipping the valet extra to bring his car around in a hurry. The teen took Stephen at his word, squealing the tires of his Jaguar as he maneuvered the sleek automobile over from the parking lot.

A lot of men would have gone into coronary arrest,

right after committing brutal, cold-blooded murder. Stephen surprised her by merely shaking his head and saying in a dry tone, "That's what I get for telling a kid to step on it when he's got the keys to my Jag."

Then he squealed the tires himself as the sleek sports coupé shot away from the curb and into night traffic. She figured out right away that they weren't going home, but he remained tight-lipped beside her, saying only, "You'll see," when she asked him their destination.

Then she saw the marquee and knew. *Charade* with Cary Grant and Audrey Hepburn was playing at an old theater that showed only vintage films, including the accompanying trailers and newsreels.

"We're going to the movies?" she asked needlessly, as he swerved to the curb and into a lucky parking space half a block from the theater. He hopped out, came around to her side of the car and all but yanked her to her feet.

"Yeah. Can you run in those heels?"

He didn't wait for her answer, but grabbed her by the hand and started off at a trot.

"Movie starts in less than a minute and I want to get popcorn." He sounded almost like a kid when he added, "They use real butter here. You like butter, right?"

Again, he didn't wait for her answer, but she didn't mind. She'd never seen Stephen like this, rushing as if his life depended on seeing a movie he'd probably already watched a dozen times. In fact, she didn't doubt he owned a copy of it, either on video or DVD. Perhaps both.

They were the only ones in the theater decked out in formal wear, but he didn't seem to mind the double-takes, raised eyebrows and whispers. He sent her to the concession stand while he purchased the tickets, and met her there just in time to pay for the king-sized bucket of buttered popcorn, beverages and Milk Duds he'd asked her to purchase.

The photograph caught her attention the moment he opened his wallet. It was of the two of them, standing side by side in the I Do Chapel. She'd forgotten about the pictures that had come with their deluxe wedding package. Apparently Stephen had not. He'd kept them, cut one down to fit the plastic protector in his wallet and carried it with him. She was ridiculously touched.

"I didn't know you had these." She pointed to the photograph.

He seemed uncomfortable when he replied, "Most married men carry pictures of their wives."

"So, it's for effect?" she asked.

He didn't answer her question, instead he said, "You looked beautiful that day." Dark eyes studied her for a moment. Then he handed her one of the drinks and a paper-covered straw. "You look beautiful every day."

Before she could respond, he hoisted the tub of popcorn into his arms and grabbed the other drink. "Don't forget the Milk Duds."

"I can't believe we're doing this," she whispered as they took their seats in the back of the theater.

"You have to admit it beats another two hours of small talk with the movers and shakers of Greater Chicago."

She dipped her hand into the tub and feasted on a mouthful of popcorn. When she was done she said, "I won't argue with a man when he's right. Do you have the napkins?"

"No, I thought you had them."

"Nope. Can I use your handkerchief, then."

"I have a better idea." As Cary Grant flirted with Audrey Hepburn on the screen, Stephen lifted Catherine's hand and one by one slowly licked the butter from her fingers.

He wasn't sure why'd he'd done it, although from the way she sucked in a breath and leaned toward him he didn't think Catherine minded. He rubbed his own buttery hands on his tuxedo pants, unmindful of the obscene price he'd paid for them. Then there was only the small matter of setting aside the popcorn tub so that he could take her face in his hands, bring it forward for the kiss. She tasted salty and incredibly sweet.

They were in the rear of a sparsely crowded theater, but they could have been front and center at a sold-out performance of a Broadway play and he doubted it would have kept him from trailing a hand down the slim column of her neck and then following it with his lips. He stopped at her collarbone and the cloth that covered it, and prayed for some sanity to return. He'd never wanted a woman the way he wanted Catherine.

"Sorry. I got carried away."

"I'll say," she whispered back.

But when he started to straighten she wound her arms around his neck. "Do you think you could get carried away again?"

His smile came slowly, despite his charging heart. "I'll see what I can do."

This time he was determined not to be deterred by clothing. He took Catherine's sexy little sigh as consent. His fingers were just starting to dip beneath the fabric of the gown's bodice when a beam of light all but blinded him. He kicked over the tub of popcorn in his haste to sit upright.

"Sir." It came out as squawk, so the teenager wielding the flashlight cleared his throat and tried again. "Sir, um, ma'am, we don't, um, you know, allow that kind of stuff in here. If you, like, keep it up, I'll have to ask you to leave."

When he was gone Catherine succumbed to a fit of laughter, and Stephen couldn't help but think that many of their acquaintances would have found it hard to reconcile this irrepressible and incredibly responsive woman with the overly regimented and cool image she often projected.

"Let's get out of here," he said.

"But the movie's not over. Don't you want to find out how it ends?"

He kissed her hard and let her go. "Oh, yeah. I want to find out how it ends."

They ran on the way back to his car, too.

On the way home they held hands, and it struck Stephen as absurd that he was essentially dating his own wife and wondering with all the hopeful anticipation of a teenager if the evening would end as well as he was imagining. He parked the Jag in the garage, but they didn't get out immediately. Both seemed to know that once they went inside everything would change.

"We're home," Catherine said needlessly after the silence had dragged and the light on the automatic garage door opener had gone dim.

"Yes." He opened the car door and the interior light popped on, haloing them in soft gold. "Shall we go inside?"

Catherine laid a hand on his arm. "Before we do, I need to know what's going on between us."

"I think it's this."

He leaned over and kissed her, and felt the jolt of that surprising attraction. His world had been careening and threatening to crash around him, but Catherine had saved him. And in the midst of chaos he'd found something special, something precious. He'd found... He rejected the thought before it was fully formed.

But it was she who ended the kiss.

"We shouldn't be doing this."

He couldn't help but smile. "We have more right than most. We are married."

"We're not really married." She straightened her clothing.

"Oh?" He arched an eyebrow. "I have a piece of paper that says otherwise."

"You know what I mean, Stephen. This isn't a love match."

"No, but I like you. I respect you. I think it's fairly obvious I'm incredibly attracted to you."

"I settled for attraction once," she whispered. "It's not enough. I like and respect you as well. And that's why I don't want to complicate things between us. My God, aren't they complicated enough?"

Much as he hated to admit it, she was right, but he wondered how long what was growing between them could be denied.

Once again he walked her to her bedroom door, leaving her there with Degas. The walk to his own room seemed as long and lonely as a walk to the gallows.

The next couple of weeks went by in a blur. Catherine didn't need to pretend to keep herself busy. Fall was always a hectic time for charities as they geared up for the holiday season, and long before she'd exchanged vows with Stephen she had committed to attend various events and fund-raisers.

She'd figured her full schedule would allow her and Stephen to give one another a wide berth, perhaps put some of their awkwardness behind them. But, to her utter amazement, Stephen always insisted on coming with her. He was a perfect gentleman, a perfect escort, with his impeccable manners and gorgeous dark looks. And, even though things remained strained between them, he never let it show when they were out in public. He would pull her close to dance, touch her shoulders a bit longer than necessary when he removed her wrap, tuck her hand into the crook of his elbow as they entered a room, and all evening he would watch her with those sizzling, sexy eyes that held too many secrets for her comfort.

Was it all just for show? Catherine didn't want to believe it was, but at home the byplay between them was limited to polite, if not awkward conversation. He'd told her that he liked and respected her. Was it possible that he could someday feel something more where she was concerned? For she feared that she was beginning to feel something much deeper for him.

She arrived home on Saturday, two grocery bags in tow, determined to try her hand at an Italian dish she'd seen in the gourmet cooking magazine to which she subscribed. When she opened the door from the garage, however, her eardrums were assaulted by Bob Seger's gritty voice. Stephen was apparently already home, even though it was barely four o'clock and he usually worked until six, even at weekends.

She followed the music until she found him. He was in a back room that he'd had converted to a weight room. Assorted sizes of dumbbells and free weights lined the walls. Stephen reclined on the slim bench, stripped to the waist in a pair of nylon shorts and pumping some serious iron. He didn't see her, so Catherine allowed herself a moment of pure ogling, and the hunger she felt had nothing to do with the fact she had skipped lunch.

So this was where he got the biceps she'd admired, not to mention the delts and pecs that did his tailored shirts proud. Oh, she would suffer some incredibly detailed fantasies in the future—and she did mean *suffer*—but it was worth it to be able to openly watch her handsome husband.

He stopped his reps and sat up, blotting the perspiration from his face with a towel he'd draped over the end of the bench. And then he saw her. He stood, switched off the blaring rock and faced her.

"Something I can help you with?"

"I didn't mean to interrupt." She motioned toward the bench. "Are you finished?"

"For now."

"They say that working out is a good way to relieve tension," she said, when he just continued to stare at her.

He stalked forward until he stood just in front of her, more than six feet of sweaty and seemingly angry male.

"I can think of better ways to relieve this kind of tension, Catherine."

He stepped around her and then he was gone.

Catherine burned dinner, but it didn't matter. Stephen had gone out shortly after their confrontation in the weight room. It was nearly midnight when Degas whined and she heard Stephen's muffled footsteps on the stairs. Again, she wondered where he'd been and whom he'd been with.

Catherine stumbled into the kitchen early the next morning, her system in need of some serious caffeine before she tackled the job of cleaning up the mess she'd made the night before. She'd been in no mood to scrub pots and pans after her disastrous dinner.

To her surprise, Stephen was already seated in the nook, dressed in casual tan pants and a cotton navy crewneck, munching on a slice of toast.

"You're up early today."

"I've decided to take *La Libertad* out for one last sail before dry-docking her for the winter."

"Hmm." She glanced toward the window and the patch of blue visible through it. "Should be a good day for it,"

Sipping his coffee, he nodded. "If the weather forecast is to be believed it's going to be sunny and unseasonably warm."

She'd hoped for an invitation, but wasn't terribly surprised when one didn't come. If the man found it difficult to spend time with her in a six-thousand-square-foot house, surely a thirty-eight-foot sailboat would be sheer torture.

"Well, have a good time."

She turned and walked to the counter to pour herself a cup of coffee, and then nearly scalded her hand when he asked, "Is it going to take you long to get ready?"

"You want me to go with you?"

"I want you...to go." He hesitated just long enough between the words to shroud his exact meaning.

"Stephen—"

He interrupted, his tone sounding sincere when he said, "I want to spend the day with you, Catherine. Just the two of us."

"I'd like that, too."

"I figured we'd swing by a deli first, have a picnic lunch packed. We can make an entire day of it, if that suits you."

An entire day aboard his sailboat, miles from shore, with no chaperones. Nothing good could come from it, her practical mind warned. Yet she found herself smiling with excitement, her blood humming with anticipation.

"It suits me."

CHAPTER EIGHT

LAKE MICHIGAN proved a gentle hostess, her waters a calm and vibrant blue that reminded Catherine of satin. The sun warmed her face and allowed her to remain comfortable in the sweater and jeans she'd worn. And the breeze co-operated as well. It ruffled the sails and tugged the boat out to where the tall buildings on the shoreline looked so small they could be covered with one's thumb.

"Are you enjoying your sail?"

With her face turned to the sun, eyes closed, she smiled. "Very much. Thank you for asking me."

"I almost didn't."

She opened her eyes and turned to look at him, but said nothing.

"I remember what happened the last time we were aboard *La Libertad*."

She'd been sure he was going to mention the night at the movie theater, when needs and desires had beckoned...threatened to overtake them. His reference to that summer evening perplexed her.

"I don't understand. Nothing happened."

"Something happened. And it wasn't the first time. I've been attracted to you for a long time, even when I didn't want to be."

132

"When I was engaged to Derek?"

"Before that."

She sat upright. "But you never said a word."

"What was I going to say? I thought it would pass, especially after you became involved with my cousin. I thought I was just attracted to the pretty packaging. You're a very beautiful woman."

And so he had told her, on more than one occasion. Derek had told her that as well, which made the compliment seem hollow, almost an insult.

"I'd like to think I'm more than that."

"You are. That's what makes you so dangerous."

"Dangerous?" She laughed, sure he was joking, but his gaze remained intense, his mouth a taut line. "I'm not dangerous, Stephen. What you see is what you get."

"Oh, no, Catherine. You're much more than what one sees or what you choose to let people see. Why is that?"

"People make assumptions. You made them yourself."

"And you let them. Why?"

She shrugged.

"Last year, Project Christmas was falling short of its goal for the first time in fifteen years. It hadn't done that poorly since the last recession. I poured on the charm, made a few phone calls to some people who can be incredibly generous when they want to be or when they're talked into it. I'm good at talking people into doing things."

"Some might call that manipulation."

She nodded in agreement. "Maybe I do manipulate people, but not for my own gain. Surely that distinction counts for something?"

"What drives you?"

"I like to make a difference." It was her standard answer, but he didn't look convinced.

"It's more than that. You could make a difference by heading a beautification committee or simply writing a check."

His assessment was uncomfortably close to her parents' way of being community-minded. She thought of that lonely, frightened little girl who had reached out for help and received only money in the form of a scholarship in return.

"It's not enough."

Again he asked, "What drives you, Catherine?"

She'd never spoken to anyone about "the incident," as her parents referred to it. At first she had been too shocked and sad. Then had come the guilt, and so she had remained silent. But for some reason it seemed safe, easy to talk about the unspeakable with Stephen.

Her voice low, halting at first, she began. "I had a friend once, a little girl named Jenny. She came from the Projects, but attended my private school thanks to a scholarship my parents had set up. She was bright, vibrant, thankful for every crumb she received when everyone else I knew just expected everything they got and even then complained."

"What happened to her?"

"I knew she had a hard home life, even though I'd never been allowed to her home. My parents forbade it. But we hung out at school and I saw the bruises. No twelve-year-old is as clumsy as Jenny claimed to be."

"What did you do about it?"

"I told my parents I thought something was wrong. Jenny seemed to become more and more withdrawn at school. Her grades started to suffer."

"What did they say?"

"They told me it wasn't my concern. A couple of weeks later Jenny was dead. She'd been beaten to death by her mother's boyfriend." Once again, Catherine felt the stab of pain and accompanying guilt. "So, you see, writing a check isn't enough, Stephen."

"You can't blame yourself. You were a child. What could you have done?"

"More," she said simply.

He frowned. "How can you stand it?"

"What?"

"Having people think you're this cool, shallow woman when you are anything but?"

"I don't care what other people think of me. I know who I am."

He came forward and knelt in front of the bench on which she sat. Taking her face between his hands, he said, "I know who you are, too, Catherine."

"You do?"

"Yes, you're my wife."

This kiss was gentle, but persuasive. She had no choice but to give in to its seductive charm. And it really was no hardship to admit defeat. She took what he offered and then surprised them both by demanding more. Urgent now, the kiss had desire pounding through her veins. Every time she told herself the excitement of his touch would dim, he surprised new emotions from her, uncovering a reservoir of need she hadn't known existed. Was it just about physical attraction? She knew it wasn't for her, and surely Stephen had just as good as admitted that his feelings ran much deeper than what basic hormonal urges would manufacture?

A gamble. That was what this had been since the beginning. Even before their wedding in Las Vegas she'd taken a chance, bet on fate. Well, roll the dice.

"Make love to me, Stephen."

He stopped his exploration of her neck. Dark eyes regarded her intently.

"That night in the car you said—"

She placed her hand over his mouth. "What I said that night isn't important. Today is a new day, and I want my *husband* to make love to me."

He stood and reached for her hand, pulling her to her feet with a gentle tug. He whispered something in Spanish, beautiful, incomprehensible words that caused her breath to hitch, her heart to ache. *I will remember this moment always,* Catherine thought.

The moment when she first tumbled headlong into love.

He led her below deck, to the larger of the two staterooms, which was still small enough to be considered cozy. He didn't say a word as he began to undress her.

"You have nice hands."

She kissed the palm of one and then the other.

And Stephen was undone. Even if he could have ignored the passion stirring in her gaze, there was no mistaking the raw desire that had turned her demure voice into the smoky whisper of a siren.

"Catherine." He closed his eyes and said her name as reverently as he would a prayer.

Seemingly of their own volition, the hands she claimed to admire traveled down her torso and then back up, pulling the bulky sweater she wore with them. He pulled it over her head and then sucked in a breath at the pale perfection of her skin, which was in striking contrast to the lacy navy bra. Then, heaven help him, Stephen couldn't stop his fingers from inching aside the lace. He heard her echo the groan that tore from his own chest before she leaned forward and fused her mouth to his. This kiss, like the one they had shared in the car that night, was wild with need. His body responded instantly.

Stephen prided himself on his finesse as a lover, but just now he felt as desperate and out-of-control as a teenager. He didn't tease and tempt her with lingering caresses and sensuous nibbles. He wanted, so he took. His mouth plundered and devoured while his eager fingers grasped and clutched and tugged away the last barriers of her clothing.

Below him on the bed, Catherine gave a sexy little moan, her own hands making fast work of ridding him of the clothing he wore.

When he was naked, and straining over her, she ran her delicate hands up his chest and then fisted them in his hair, pulling him down for another hot kiss.

"Now." She breathed the word into his mouth. "Please, now."

"Say my name," he commanded, using every ounce of self-control to pull back just far enough so he could look at her. "I want to hear you say my name."

He watched her lips curve into a smile that was sensual and oddly shy. "Stephen," she whispered.

That was all it took. One word. His name. He brought their bodies together quickly, the need so fierce it astounded him. This kind of passion, this kind of emotional connection represented uncharted territory. Below him, Catherine responded, rhythm matching rhythm, need matching need, heat matching heat until they were both flung over the edge of sanity on a shattering climax. On the freefall back to earth he heard her call out his name again.

Then, using the language only those most dear spoke to him in, she whispered, *"Mi amor."*

Afterward, he rolled to his side and gathered her to

his chest, where she settled one hand over his still hammering heart. It felt for all the world as if she belonged there in the loose circle of his arms, her body limp from release, her head tucked trustingly beneath his chin. And the raging need he'd felt a moment earlier gentled into something far more disturbing.

The gulls woke him. Their irritating squawks blasted rudely through his dreams and had Stephen rolling onto his side, arm outstretched and seeking the warm, curved comfort of a woman's body. It came into contact with cool cotton and nothing more. He sat up and blinked in sleepy confusion at the rumpled sheets.

"Catherine?"

He found her puttering in the little kitchen, humming in that endearing off-key way of hers. She wore only his shirt, and he thought she looked sexier than a lingerie model. She had placed the sandwiches they'd bought at the deli on plates and was doling out pasta salad when he came up behind her and scooped her hair aside so he could kiss the back of her neck.

"Hmm. I like that."

"I've noticed," he replied, still amazed by what a responsive woman lurked beneath her quiet composure.

She turned, looped her arms around his neck and kissed him with a greedy passion that one would not suspect from such an otherwise generous woman.

"I seem to have worked up an appetite."

"Me, too," he agreed, as he began to unbutton his big shirt to reveal the feminine perfection beneath it.

It was another hour before they sat down in the cozy kitchen to eat their lunch.

The day was ending, Catherine knew. The magical, wonderful hours were drawing to a close. She wanted them to last, worried that once she and Stephen returned to dry land whatever spell the beautiful waters of Lake Michigan had cast would be broken, and if that happened she knew her heart would shatter as well.

The wind had picked up, making quick work of their sail back to the yacht club. Once there, she helped him unload their gear from the day. Then she waited in the car while he made arrangements for the boat to be stored for the winter.

"Are you tired?" he asked as they drove home.

"Exhausted," she said with an exaggerated yawn. "Can't imagine why."

"There's someone I'd like you to meet."

She straightened in her seat. "Now?"

"It's on the way home."

"Who?"

"My grandmother."

Catherine wanted to meet his family. She knew what his grandmother meant to him. The woman had been like a surrogate mother, giving him the love and encouragement the Danburys had withheld, filling in the blanks of his rich heritage. Oh, yes, she wanted to meet her. But right now?

"Oh, Stephen. My hair is a mess and I..." she flipped down the visor to check her reflection in the mirror. Tilting her head to one side, she blanched. "Oh, my God! Is that a whisker burn?"

He chuckled. "My grandmother is near-sighted. Don't worry."

"Oh, but look how I'm dressed." Her clothes were rumpled from an afternoon spent on the floor of the stateroom.

"My grandmother won't be offended. There's no need to dress for dinner at her house. It's a casual affair, believe me."

"Dinner? She's having us for dinner and you never said a word about the invitation before now?"

"It's a standing invitation. She makes enough for an army every Sunday. Whoever stops by is welcome."

"Who else stops by?"

"My aunts, cousins, their families." He shrugged.

"They'll all be there?"

"Some of them, sure."

"You said before that they knew about our arrangement. I'll feel...awkward in their presence."

"They know about our arrangement," he acknowledged. "They also know I would never bring someone I didn't care about to dinner." He took her hand, kissed the back of it. "I want you to meet my family, Catherine. Will you do me the honor?"

When he put it like that, she couldn't refuse.

"It's me who is honored, Stephen."

His grandmother's house was not especially large, nor was it in an exclusive neighborhood. But there was no denying its charm. With its stone façade, it reminded her of a fairy-tale cottage. Chrysanthemums bloomed like pots of gold in the flower beds, where other perennials had already enjoyed their glory and had now been cut back in preparation for winter.

The instant they stepped across the threshold they were surrounded by boisterous, enthusiastic relatives of varying ages and sizes, all chattering excitedly. Some spoke in English, some in Spanish. All with the kind of welcoming fondness that Catherine had thought only Hollywood could manufacture. She was kissed and hugged by people she had never met before and whose names had already become confused.

"Welcome, welcome," a plump older woman said, wiping her hands on an apron as she crossed the room to where they stood just inside the door. It was as far as they had gotten before being surrounded by family members.

"*Abuelita,*" Stephen said with a grin. "I'd like you to meet Catherine. Catherine, this is my grandmother, Consuela Fuentes."

"It's nice to meet you, Señora Fuentes," Catherine said. She had barely gotten the words out when she was wrapped in a pair of surprisingly strong arms and soundly kissed on both cheeks.

"You will call me *Abuelita*, yes?"

"Abuelita." She tried out the word, liking the way it sounded. Stephen's family nodded their approval.

Throughout their visit it became clear to Catherine that while Stephen had grown up in privilege, surrounded by servants and wealthy grandparents who had been miserly with their affection, here he had known generous helpings of love. There was no sign of the aloof, intense man in Consuela Fuentes's homey living room. He wrestled on the floor with his cousins' children, joked with his uncles, complimented his aunts.

Dinner was a casual affair, the food not as spicy as Catherine had thought it would be, but filling and delicious and made in massive quantities. People laughed and talked, sometimes over one another, passing serving bowls or even hopping up to walk down to the far end of the table for what they wanted. It was informal, bordering on chaotic. It was fantastic.

From all of the chatter Catherine deduced that the evenings when Stephen had slipped away, not to return till late, had been spent here.

Afterward, when the last bit of dessert had been eaten, Catherine helped Stephen's three aunts and grandmother clear the table. They wouldn't let her help wash the dishes, but she sat on a stool at the counter in the kitchen and listened to them chatter happily about babies and bargains, the lyrical cadence of their voices making even the mundane seem magical. And she knew if not for her presence much of the conversation would have been conducted in Spanish and more than likely would have centered on her.

"Christina and Miguel are expecting again. They are hoping for a boy this time." For Catherine's benefit Rosaria added, "They already have four daughters."

Miguel was Stephen's cousin and Rosaria's oldest son. From the introductions, and from listening to the conversations, Catherine thought she had all the relationships down.

Stephen's grandmother had four daughters, including Stephen's mother, Galena, who had been the oldest. Rosaria was the second oldest, then came Rita and Selena. All of the daughters, with the exception of Galena, had married men from their native Puerto Rico or men who were Hispanic. Most of their children were grown now, with families of their own.

"When will you and Stephen start a family?" Rosaria asked.

The question startled Catherine enough that she spilt her tea. A family? They had not planned to start a family. They had not planned to remain married. But surely after today, after that wonderful afternoon of making love, things had changed?

CHAPTER NINE

A BITTER wind whipped through downtown Chicago, stealing pedestrians' breath and turning their cheeks more ruddy red than rosy. It was barely November, but the chilly temperatures heralded the long winter to come. Even so, Stephen was whistling as he entered the Danbury Building and headed to the elevators. It had been an incredible month, and now another weekend was drawing near. An absolutely free weekend. He and Catherine had no charity functions to attend, nothing that required their presence.

Since the afternoon on *La Libertad*, she had spent every night in his bed, and he figured this weekend would be as good a time as any to move the rest of her things into the master suite. That was where she belonged. Near him. Next to him. In his bed just as surely as she was in his heart.

It still frightened him, this need, this…love. He'd never felt anything quite so overpowering, quite so consuming. Or, he admitted, quite so fulfilling.

His fingers closed around the small velvet box in the pocket of his overcoat. Inside it was the ring he planned to give Catherine that night, to replace the cheap one they'd bought in Las Vegas. This was not just any ring, but the one his father had given his mother: a flawless two-carat marquis-cut diamond surrounded by sapphires. He'd just come from the jewelers, where it had been cleaned and resized based on another ring he'd found in Catherine's jewelry box.

He would give it to her after dinner, maybe even get down on one knee and propose. They could renew their vows, maybe even have a real wedding this time, complete with all the trimmings she'd missed out on in Las Vegas. She'd like that. She was such a romantic.

Life was good, he decided, and then nearly took it back when Derek stepped into the elevator just before the doors closed.

"What are you doing here?"

"It is the Danbury Building, and I am a Danbury. More of a Danbury, I might add, than you'll ever be, *Stefano*."

"You have no business here. You're no longer an executive with the company. The new vice president starts next week."

"Yes, Sam Maxwell from the Hartford store. As by-the-book as they come," he sneered.

"Which means he'll actually do some work to earn his keep," Stephen countered.

"What's Catherine doing to earn her keep?"

"Don't go there," Stephen warned, as fury vibrated through his system.

"So touchy."

"I won't discuss my wife with you."

"Well, a word to the wise, *cousin*, her family's broke."

"The economy has been hard on a lot of people, Derek. That's no newsflash."

"It's been harder on the Cantons than most. Your in-laws are mortgaged to the hilt. And you know how Catherine likes to help people out."

"Catherine's family is no concern of yours."

"Yes, you're right. In fact even if we had married they would have been none of my concern. They might have thought I was going to be their meal ticket, but I knew better. And I was smart enough to make Catherine sign a prenuptial agreement. Somehow I doubt that in your rush to the altar you got around to that," Derek drawled.

"Again, it's none of your concern."

Derek laughed. "I thought as much. No prenup." He tsked. "You are a fool. What if you wind up losing Danbury's anyway? Or at least half of it to her in a divorce settlement?"

"You're wrong about her. Catherine's no gold-digger. She's not like that."

"*All* women are like that," Derek replied. "And Catherine has more reason to be than most. After all, by marrying you she's already proved the old adage about hell having no fury like a woman scorned."

"You don't know anything about our marriage."

"Come now, don't tell me you have feelings for her? You were never more than a rebound to

Catherine, a way for her to get even with me. And, I'll admit it, she has. You both have.''

''This is no longer about you.'' Maybe it never was, Stephen thought now.

The elevator doors opened and he stepped out. But before the doors could slide shut again Derek held out a hand to stop them and said, ''Don't tell me you think she loves you? A few months ago she loved me. She probably still does.''

''You don't love her. You never loved her.''

''I love the half of the company a shrewd lawyer could help her take from you in a divorce.''

Again he laughed, setting Stephen's teeth on edge, and, worse, introducing a niggling seed of doubt. Could Catherine still have feelings for Derek?

''Even if she left me she'd never take you back. Not after what she witnessed in the church.''

''We'll see. But in the meantime she's in a very good position to take you to the cleaners. And, should that happen, I'll be only too happy to begin seeing her again.''

''You're delusional.''

''I don't know.'' Derek offered a dazzling smile. ''I've been told I can be very charming. I believe Cherise Langston told me that just last night. You remember Cherise?''

Stephen shook his head in disgust. The pair of them deserved one another.

''If you're attempting to make me jealous it won't work. Cherise was a lovely distraction for a brief time, but nothing more. If you want to talk about gold-diggers, I think she qualifies.''

Derek merely shrugged.

"Give Catherine my best."

He let the doors slide shut, whistling the same tune Stephen had been just moments before, and taking with him a good portion of the joy Stephen had been feeling.

Catherine was in the kitchen when Stephen got home. He offered her a smile as he absently patted Degas's broad head. She knew him well enough after these past several weeks to know when something was wrong. He seemed distracted—edgy, even.

She had planned a romantic and intimate dinner, and had spent the better part of three hours preparing and cooking it. The sautéed scallops with leeks and lemon butter sauce were already on the dining room table, along with a salad of mixed greens and fresh rolls she'd picked up at the bakery. A glance at the clock told her the pork loin was ready.

"You're just in time for dinner. I thought we'd eat in the dining room tonight."

"Hmm? Uh, sure. That's fine."

"Why don't you change your clothes and pour yourself a drink? I'll put this on a serving tray and join you in a moment."

He nodded.

A few minutes later Stephen entered the dining room, clad in casual trousers and an oxford. He'd been only too glad to shed his suit and tie. If only his mood were as easy to change. He glanced at the flickering candles in the middle of the dining room table. He thought about the romantic evening he'd had planned, and the ring he'd stashed away in a drawer upstairs. He hated to let his cousin ruin his plans. Indeed, he'd once admonished Catherine for allowing Derek to raise suspicions and stir up trouble. But the doubt was there, as well as the old insecurity.

Maybe it was too soon to talk about love and life-long commitments. After all, under normal circumstances they would just be in the beginning stages of dating. So far they'd gotten everything backward. They'd married and then begun a courtship. They knew each other's living habits without knowing each other's hearts. Perhaps if things moved more slowly, built up more gradually, as they would in a normal relationship. The ring could wait, he decided.

"What's bothering you?" Catherine asked when she joined him in the dining room.

He shrugged. "Why do you think something is bothering me?"

"You just seem like you've got a lot on your mind. Work going okay?"

"The same." He rubbed a hand across his brow. "Profits look to be down again this quarter."

"It's the economy. Everyone is feeling the pinch. People are scaling back on purchases. But Thanksgiving is right around the corner, and then the

Christmas shopping season will kick into high gear. Things will turn around.''

He smiled and reached out to take her hand.

''Is this a pep talk?''

''Is it working?''

''I'll let you know.'' He tugged on her hand, pulling until she left her seat and settled sideways on his lap. He tried to keep the urgency out of his kiss, but the desperate need he felt for validation must have slipped in.

''Are you sure everything is all right?'' she asked.

''It's...been a long day, and what I really want right now is you.''

She smiled, that odd little dimple denting in her cheek. ''Well, you have me.''

Do I? The question went unspoken, though. He kissed her instead, deeply, passionately, until they were both breathless and more than a little aroused.

''This chair isn't adequate for what I have in mind.'' He tilted her head to the side, nibbled her neck. ''What do you say we go upstairs?''

''What about dinner? You haven't even sampled my scallops yet.''

''I'd rather sample you.''

Her blouse was a wrap style and he had no trouble removing it. Before Catherine could fathom what he meant to do she found herself divested of it, and the silk camisole underneath, and perched on the edge of the dining room table in the exact spot where Stephen's place setting had been. The china had been pushed back, along with her skirt. Its hem now rode the tops of thighs, offering a glimpse of the lacy white garters that held up her sheer stockings.

He hooked an index finger beneath one of the fasteners and said, ''What have we here?''

He hadn't seemed hungry a minute ago, but now he looked absolutely ravenous, and Catherine rather doubted her well-seasoned pork loin had anything to do with it. Indeed, the culinary feast she had painstakingly prepared had been crossed off her own list of priorities.

''I was planning to buy a cheesecake for dessert, but I splurged on some new lingerie instead. Do you like it?''

''I haven't seen it. Not all of it, anyway.''

''Let's go upstairs.''

''Uh-uh.'' One side of his mouth lifted in a smile. ''I've changed my mind. Let's stay here.''

He reached behind her and undid the hook on her skirt, then pulled the zipper as low as the table would allow. She scooted off the edge and stood. The skirt slid down her legs and puddled at her feet. She should have been embarrassed to be standing in the dining room wearing nothing but a snowy white thong, garter belt, sheer stockings and black high heels, but the look on Stephen's face made her feel empowered instead.

Catherine thought about the many fantasies she'd entertained since their marriage. And, even though she had no complaints about their lovemaking, she couldn't dismiss the excitement she felt just now.

"I've never made love in a dining room before."

"I can't say that I ever have either. Is that an invitation?"

She smiled, only too glad to give the order. "Take off your clothes."

Dinner grew cold even as the temperature in the room spiked to sizzling.

Later that night, as Catherine slept beside him, Stephen thought about Derek's allegations. He wouldn't believe them, he decided. Even as he made this vow, however, he couldn't quite escape the worry that somehow his cousin would manage to best him again. All their lives Derek—the golden boy with the classic Danbury looks—had come out ahead. He had been doted on by their grandparents and eyed by debutantes' mothers as Stephen had stood on the sidelines and watched.

Derek claimed to be charming, and indeed he was. His smooth manners, charismatic smile and good looks hid his egocentric nature. Could his cousin persuade Catherine that he still loved her? She had fallen under the spell of his charm once. Could she again?

When morning broke he still wasn't sure he knew the answers.

Catherine stared at the small stick and reread the instructions that had come with the test kit. There was no mistake. She was pregnant. She laid her hands on her flat stomach, stared at her reflection in the bathroom mirror and grinned, happier than she could ever remember being.

She didn't have to wonder when she had conceived. That day aboard *La Libertad* had been the only time they'd made love without protection. After that they'd always had something nearby. Even a week earlier in the dining room they'd shown admirable restraint until a condom could be slipped on.

She chuckled at the care they had taken during the past several weeks. As it turned out none of it had mattered after that magical sailing trip on Lake Michigan. A baby was growing inside of her. Stephen's baby.

She would tell him that night. Maybe light a few candles, pour some champagne. Champagne? She laughed out loud. No, no, not champagne. She was expecting a child now. She couldn't be drinking alcohol. They would toast this new life with sparkling grape juice. Then Stephen would take her in his arms, kiss her and tell her how much he loved her.

Her smile faltered and the fantasy dissolved. He had yet to say the words. And, oh, how Catherine wanted the words. Now more than ever she needed to hear them, especially since he had seemed so preoccupied in recent days. Sometimes she would catch him looking at her, as if trying to decipher the answer to something that puzzled and troubled him greatly. Whenever she asked what was wrong his answer was always the same: nothing. But something was bothering him. Could it be he regretted that their relationship had changed? Maybe as much as he enjoyed her company he still wanted his freedom at the end of the year.

No, he loved her, her heart insisted. Surely he had told her so in dozens of other ways—with searing kisses, gentle caresses, thoughtful comments and quiet conversations in the dark as they cuddled in his bed after making love. All of those things mattered more than the actual words. Even so, she decided she would wait to hear him declare his feelings before telling him about the baby.

"Want to watch a movie tonight?" she asked as they ate dinner that night.

"*The Maltese Falcon?*"

She wrinkled her nose. That wasn't what she had in mind at all.

"I was thinking *Sabrina*, the original version."

She wanted moonlight and yearning, passion and romance. She wanted a happy ending. Not only for Audrey Hepburn's character, but for herself.

He shrugged. "I guess I can sit through it."

"Ah, chivalry. Who says it's dead?"

He helped her clear the table and load the dishwasher. She was humming a popular ballad when she glanced over and caught him smiling.

"What's so funny?"

"I enjoy hearing you sing."

"I know I don't have a good voice. Felicity says I couldn't carry a tune if it came with handles."

He kissed the tip of her nose. "I enjoy hearing you sing," he said again.

And he did, Stephen decided. Off-key as could be, and yet there was something perfect about the way she slaughtered a song as she puttered in their kitchen. *It had to be love.* Why else would such an assault on his ears also be endearing?

Again, he knew a moment of panic. What if she didn't feel it, too? The signs were there that she did. The glances, the way she casually touched the back of his hand during conversation. She tucked her body close to his in sleep, called his office during the day for no reason at all. Still Derek's words haunted him. For the first time in his life Stephen had opened his heart, and he couldn't bear the thought that the woman he loved might not love him in return.

Catherine was still humming, oblivious to his concerns. But he needed a moment to put his old demons back where they belonged.

"I'll go get the movie ready while you finish up in here."

Catherine settled onto the couch in what Stephen had dubbed the entertainment room. It had a large flat-screen television, with movie-theater-quality picture and sound, and everything from dimming the lights to controlling the room's temperature could done with the push of a button on a large remote control. The room had its own refrigerator, stocked with soft drinks, beer and mixers, a liquor cabinet, and a microwave for making popcorn, even though Stephen always insisted that the best popcorn was made in a pot on the stove and then smothered in real melted butter.

"Popcorn tonight?" he asked, as he slid the movie into the VCR—he didn't have this one on DVD yet—and began to fast-forward through the trailers and credits.

"No, thanks. I'm too full from dinner to eat anything else."

"Wine, then? I picked up a nice Merlot on the way home from work."

"I'll pass."

"It's that Merlot you told me you wanted to try last week."

"Oh. Well, the fact is I've decided to give it up wine altogether. It, um, makes me too sleepy."

Stephen couldn't have said why, but he didn't think she was telling the truth. But why would she lie over something as insignificant as not wanting a glass of wine?

As the weeks passed, though, it seemed to Stephen that Catherine was using all sorts of small lies and evasions. He swore she was hiding something. And, whatever it was, it seemed to be taking its toll on her health. She was often tired—nodding off as they watched a movie, yawning through dinner.

Sometimes he arrived home from work to find her napping. And her appetite had fled as well. Food she had once loved seemed to hold no appeal for her, and sometimes she looked positively green.

"Must be the flu," she told him.

She'd had the "flu" four times that week.

He worried that she could be seriously ill, but she insisted she was fine, just busy because of the holiday season. But then he came home one day to find a message on their answering machine from a doctor's office, reminding her of an appointment the next day. He waited for her to mention it, to confide in him about whatever was going on. But she merely picked at her dinner that evening and then went to bed early.

Stephen sat up with a glass of Scotch and Humphrey Bogart for company.

Catherine felt the strain of keeping her secret. She longed to tell Stephen about this new life growing inside her, to share her excitement and first pregnancy trepidation. But as one day passed into the next Stephen seemed no closer to expressing his feelings. Worse than that, he seemed to be pulling back. Oh, he was courteous and polite. She could never fault his manners. But he was killing her with each reserved please and thank you that he uttered. Their relationship seemed to be spinning back in time, instead of progressing forward.

As the icy winds of December battered Chicago, she despaired. Would she ever be able to thaw her husband's heart?

CHAPTER TEN

WITH her doctor's approval—indeed, encouragement—Catherine continued to visit the health spa
three times a week, eschewing weights and high-
impact aerobics for walking the track or swimming
laps in the pool. She usually went in the mornings,
before heading to the office, so it surprised her to run
into Marguerite on this particular Monday morning.
The other woman was not known for rising before
ten, and even though they had both belonged to the
club for years they only rarely ran across one another.
It was just Catherine's luck they would have to run
across one another on this day.

She was just finishing up five miles on the indoor
track when she heard her name come over the public
address system.

"Will Mrs. Danbury please come to the front desk?"

Catherine blotted her face with the white towel she
had draped around her neck and headed downstairs
from the elevated track that ringed the interior of the
building and afforded members a pleasantly distract-
ing view of most of the facility.

Turning the corner, she nearly collided with
Marguerite, who was coming from one of the aerobics
rooms.

The two women eyed one another warily.

"Catherine."

"Hello, Marguerite."

"Here trying to keep your figure?" She didn't wait for an answer. "Smart girl. Men soon lose interest in a woman who lets herself go after saying 'I do.' And it looks like you've put on a few pounds."

Catherine dismissed the nasty remark. She had not gained so much as a pound, despite her pregnancy. "I haven't heard Stephen complain."

"Not yet. But he will, dear. Trust me. You should talk to Len. He's the club's most requested personal trainer. He's a real taskmaster, but he does get results."

Marguerite put her hands on her own trim waist and offered a smile made no less catty by the fact her tight face barely moved.

"Oh, I thought you owed your figure to Dr. Redmond?" Catherine replied innocently, noting the name of a well-known plastic surgeon whose specialties were tummy tucks and breast augmentation.

Marguerite's gaze turned glacial. "Excuse me, I was paged."

Catherine smiled. She felt small but somehow satisfied to point out, "Or it could be me. I'm Mrs. Danbury as well."

She let Marguerite stalk off ahead of her, humming as she followed. When they reached the desk, a harried young woman glanced up. Brittney, her name tag read, and she looked to be fresh from high school.

New to the job, no doubt, and left for the first time to cover the front desk on her own.

"Can I help you?"

"I was paged," Marguerite said, raising her chin just enough to look down her professionally sculpted nose at the young woman.

"One of us was paged." Catherine offered a warm smile. "I am Catherine Danbury and this is Marguerite Danbury."

"Oh." The young woman frowned for a moment before her expression brightened. "It must be the younger Mrs. Danbury."

But Catherine didn't have long to enjoy Marguerite's irritation at the unintentional slight. Brittney held out a video. *"Yoga for Mothers-to-Be.* Tanya said to give this to you," she added, offering the name of the club's yoga instructor.

"Thanks." She was sure her face was flaming, even as the speculation burned in Marguerite's eyes.

"Expecting, are we?"

"That's really none of your business."

"No reason to be so touchy. When does the blessed event occur?"

"Again, none of your business."

"I wonder…"

"What's that supposed to mean?" she asked, but she knew what was going through the other woman's shrewd mind.

"Nothing, my dear. Not a thing."

*   *   *

Marguerite left the health club with a plot already hatching. She and Derek might never get their hands on Danbury's, as they had once schemed to do, but neither Stephen nor Catherine deserved to be happy after ruining their well-laid plans.

Revenge was sweetest when you shared it with someone. So she told her driver to take her to her son's apartment building. She didn't bother to have the doorman announce her. She used her key to access the penthouse elevator and let herself up, not bothering to wonder if Derek would be home or in the mood for unexpected visitors.

It was not quite nine in the morning when she stepped off the elevator. She headed straight for her son's bedroom, barging in on a scene that most mothers hoped to avoid.

A naked woman shrieked, diving for the sheets. Derek covered himself as well, but his expression was one of irritation rather than mortification.

"Is it too much to ask that you at least call first, Mother? I have my own home for a reason."

"Yes, well, this couldn't wait." She turned her attention to the quivering woman. "Get up, child, and get out. I need to speak to my son in private."

The woman emerged from the bed, wearing the top sheet like a toga.

"I'll call you later, Cherise," Derek said.

Cherise glared at him over her shoulder as she made her way to the bathroom, scooping up her clothing as she went. "I don't think I'll be home."

"Touchy," Marguerite commented as the bathroom door slammed shut.

"I wonder why?" Derek drawled. He pointed toward the living room. "Give me a minute, Mother."

Five minutes after an indignant Cherise had stalked out Derek emerged, freshly showered and fully clothed.

Marguerite forgave him for keeping her waiting. She was in too good a mood to let anything spoil it. She'd even made coffee, a chore she preferred to leave to the domestics. But Derek didn't employ any on a full-time basis.

"Now, what is so important that you had to roust me out of bed?"

"It's not as if you were sleeping."

"That's precisely my point."

"I ran into Catherine at the health spa this morning."

She sipped her coffee and Derek waited, knowing his mother would get to the point in her own good time.

"It seems your ex is going to have a baby."

"Are you expecting me to offer my congratulations to the happy couple?"

Unable to properly frown, she shook her head. "You disappointment me, Derek. For someone who has been looking for a way to cause problems, you should be able to see the golden opportunity presented here."

"How far along is she?"

"She wouldn't say. Very tight-lipped about the whole thing, which makes a person wonder." She managed something akin to a smile.

"Sorry to disappoint you, Mother, but you're not going to be a grandma yet. Catherine and I didn't enjoy much of a physical relationship, and when we did I was very careful—as always."

"Whether the child is yours or not doesn't matter. What Stephen thinks, however, does."

Derek grinned as her meaning apparently sank in. Setting his coffee aside, he stood.

"I trust you'll let yourself out when you're done with your coffee?"

"Where are you going?"

"I thought I would pay my dear cousin a visit."

Stephen was in a foul mood. He shuffled through the report on his desk, hoping for better news, better numbers. The holiday shopping season was in full swing, but sales were still sluggish thanks to a soft economy. Danbury's had already been running huge sales and promotions just to lure in price-conscious consumers. At this point they might as well be giving the merchandise away. Other retailers were in the same boat, but there was little comfort in having company to share the misery. He'd hoped for a profitable season. Danbury's future might well depend on it.

Just when he thought the day could not get worse,

Derek walked through the door unannounced. Stephen's harried-looking secretary scurried in behind him and offered an apologetic smile.

"It's all right, Lottie. Come in, Derek." As his cousin plopped down into one of the chairs and crossed an ankle over one knee, Stephen added sarcastically, "Have a seat and make yourself comfortable."

When they were alone, Stephen asked, "So, what brings you out at—" he consulted his watch "—ten-forty on a Monday morning? You didn't believe in rising before noon when you worked here."

"This is social. A friendly little family visit."

Stephen snorted. "We're not friends, Derek. And you don't even like to admit we're family. Why are you here? Trust fund run out already?"

"Actually, I came by to congratulate you."

Stephen eyed him suspiciously. "For what?"

"The baby, of course. You and Catherine must be thrilled."

Baby? Stephen somehow managed to keep his expression neutral, despite the throbbing in his temples. His cousin had to be wrong. This had to be one of his petty little mind games.

"And you heard about this how?"

"Mother told me. She ran into Catherine at the health club this morning and learned about it then."

He didn't buy it for a moment. It couldn't be true. Catherine would have told him. She wouldn't have kept something this monumental to herself.

Even as he told himself this he realized it all made sense. The queasiness. The fatigue. Her sudden objection to drinking wine. He knew a moment of pure joy. A baby. A family. But then the wariness returned, accompanied by the doubts that pecked at him like a flock of hostile crows.

"And you're just here to congratulate me?" His mind was reeling, but he decided to play along until he knew exactly what Derek was after. "That's very big of you."

"I'll admit when I heard about it I wondered if it could be mine. We weren't always careful, if you know what I mean. You never know..." Derek let the thought hang out there as he smiled his serpentine smile. "Of course I'm sure Catherine would never have agreed to marry you if she thought she was pregnant with my child."

Derek watched his cousin's face pale. Direct hit. Oh, to be a fly on the wall in the Stephen Danbury domicile that night. If it went as he hoped, accusations would fly and hateful things would be said. And when it was all done Derek would be there to pick up the pieces.

Deciding not to overplay his advantage, he rose. "Well, I won't keep you. I know how busy you are. Kiss the mother-to-be for me, will you?" Then he couldn't resist adding, "On that cute little mole of hers."

When he had gone Stephen slouched back in his

chair, his mind busily trying to process all the information and the not so subtle accusation his cousin had made. Was Catherine really pregnant? She didn't look it, but then they hadn't been very intimate lately. Why hadn't she told him? Could it be, as Derek insinuated, that Stephen was not the father? He didn't want to believe that, but the more he thought about it the more it seemed to make sense. What other reason would she have for keeping something like that secret?

Stephen was waiting when she got home, sitting on the living room couch, nursing his fourth Scotch. His mood had grown more volatile with each sip, shifting from melancholy to simmering rage. Norah Jones sang a haunting melody in the background. And, since he hadn't bothered with the lights, the room had grown dim along with winter's short day.

"You're home." She smiled warily, gaze sliding to the glass he held. "Bad day?"

"I've had better."

"I'm sorry to hear that. I thought we could try that new Greek restaurant tonight. I have a craving for feta cheese."

"I'll bet," he muttered.

"Excuse me?"

He took another sip and said nothing.

Her expression turned uncertain. "I guess we don't need to go out, but I didn't plan anything for dinner.

Give me an hour, though, and I can probably whip up something. Anything in particular you want?''

She walked to him and bent to kiss his mouth. He turned his head and her lips brushed his cheek instead.

Catherine knew something was seriously wrong even before he grabbed her wrist as she started to straighten and in a glacial voice demanded, "You can tell me the truth."

She pulled her hand free and backed up a step. "I don't know what you mean."

But of course she did, and her heart squeezed most painfully at this glowering expression. This was not how she wanted to tell him about the life they had created together that one wonderful afternoon aboard *La Libertad*. Not when he looked so remote, so cold, so far removed from the love she had wanted to believe had begun to blossom in his heart.

"Come now, Catherine." His voice was low, dangerous, and the rolling of the R caused her to shiver, as if the frosty wind pressing insistently against the windowpane had somehow won entry into the room.

"Tell me about the *happy* event that should be taking place in a matter of months."

He drained his glass, setting it down none too gently on the coffee table. Catherine jumped, surprised by the anger he barely managed to suppress. She had never dreamed he would be furious about his impending fatherhood.

"Stephen, I—"

"Tell me!"

"We're having a baby," she whispered, as the tears blurred her vision.

"We?" His tone was mocking, and it tore at her already battered heart.

"I know it wasn't part of our...arrangement." The word tasted bitter in her mouth. She'd been so sure there was more to their relationship than an impersonal business deal set to expire the following summer.

"It wasn't. It changes nothing," he said. As he stood, he repeated, "Nothing."

Catherine fell back a step, grateful for the overstuffed chair she sank into when her knees grew weak.

"Nothing?"

"That's what I said and that's what you'll get when the year is up. Nothing. I won't change the terms of our deal now."

"You think this is about money, Stephen? You think I planned this baby?"

"I'm sure you didn't plan it, or you probably would have gone ahead with your wedding to Derek."

"Derek? What has Derek got to do with—?"

But then she understood, and what hope she'd had that she could win her husband's heart withered like an orchid struck by frost.

The tears came, and she let them course unchecked down her cheeks. She cried for herself and for her baby, but she also cried for him. Would he never learn to trust, to love?

"Oh, Stephen, no. You think this baby is Derek's?"

"Why else wouldn't you tell me, Catherine? Why else would you keep something this important so secret that the person from whom I had to find out was my own cousin?"

She closed her eyes, imagining just how much Derek would have relished his role as messenger. "I'm sorry for that."

"I don't want your apology. I want to know why."

Talking about love seemed pointless now. He'd made up his mind not to believe her. That much was clear. "My reason doesn't matter anymore."

"I think I'm entitled to an explanation. You owe me that much." He said something in Spanish, and, given his harsh tone, she was grateful her knowledge of the language was limited. "I thought I knew you, Catherine."

"Yes, and I thought I knew you as well. I guess we were both wrong." She stood, wiped away the tears as she came to the only decision she could under the circumstances. "I'll be leaving in the morning."

"The year's not up, Catherine."

"I can't stay here. Not when you think so little of me. You once admonished me for letting Derek stir up doubts and suspicions. You're nothing but a hypocrite. The first time he hisses some venom into your ear about me you believe it."

"Give me a reason not to," he said quietly. And she didn't doubt his sincerity.

"The thing is, Stephen, I shouldn't have to."

Stephen watched her walk up the stairs with that quiet grace and dignity he had long admired. He was the wronged party here, and yet her tears had seemed real, the heartache shimmering in her sapphire eyes authentic.

He wanted to go to her. Plead with her to stay, to love him. But pride kept him planted in his seat. He'd long ago learned that you could not force people to have feelings for you. He watched her turn to the right at the top of the stairs. They seemed to have come full circle, from strangers to lovers to lovers estranged.

When he heard her bedroom door snap shut he stood, picked up his glass, and, palming it like a baseball, threw it at the fireplace. It crashed against the marble surround, shattering into dangerous jagged pieces that mocked his heart and matched his mood.

"Why?"

Stephen wasn't asleep when he heard his door open. Light from the hallway spilled inside, silhouetting Catherine's image for a moment before she stepped over the threshold. He rolled to his side and switched on the bedside lamp. If she had come to try to seduce him into changing his mind about her she wasn't dressed for the part. The conservative robe she wore was tightly belted and pulled closed at the lapels. Her expression, he noted, was pinched, pained, as if she could no longer hide her distaste for him and what she was about to do.

Even as his body made a liar of him he opened his mouth to tell her he didn't want her. But halfway to the bed she doubled over.

"Stephen!" she cried.

He shot from beneath the sheets, scooping her up into his arms before she could crumple onto the floor.

Heart hammering, he asked, "My God, what is it? What's wrong?"

"The baby." Catherine squeezed her eyes shut, the pain in her heart much greater than the pain radiating through her abdomen. She couldn't lose this baby. She just couldn't. It would be all she had of the man she loved.

He laid her gently on the bed they had shared for the past several weeks. She rolled to her side, pulling her legs up close to her body.

"I'm bleeding," she whispered, the horror as fresh as the crimson blood she'd discovered an hour earlier.

"I'll take you to the hospital."

"No."

But he was already pulling on a pair of pants. As he shoved his arms through the sleeves of a shirt he said, "Maybe I should call an ambulance?"

"No."

Shirt unbuttoned, hands falling to the side, he said, "Tell me what to do and I'll do it."

His voice was soft, pleading, and for a moment she

almost gave in to his request. Love me, she thought. Just love me. But even in her agony she could not beg him. It wasn't about pride, for if stripping herself of pride were the answer she would have done so without hesitation. But love had to be given freely, without prompting, without limitations, for it to mean anything.

The telephone rang.

"That will be the doctor," she told him. "I had his service page him."

Stephen snapped up the phone. "Hello!"

Catherine held out her hand for the receiver, but he shook his head and sat down on the edge of the bed.

"The doctor wants to know when the bleeding started."

"About an hour ago."

He relayed the information and then asked, "Is it heavy? Are you experiencing any cramping?"

"It's not too heavy, but I'm having some cramping."

He told the doctor that as well. It seemed absurd to keep up this three-way conversation, but she was too frightened to insist he hand her the telephone. She didn't want to go through this alone. If this were the only way he would be involved in her pregnancy, she would let him.

"I see," Stephen said. And then, "Yes, I'll have her in your office first thing in the morning. Thank you, Doctor."

"There's nothing we can do, is there?" Catherine

slumped back against the pillow, her eyes filling with tears.

"I'm sorry, Catherine."

His hand was gentle as it brushed the hair back from her face. He wiped away a teardrop and caressed her cheek.

"I worked out today. The doctor said I could. He said I was perfectly healthy. Maybe I did too much?"

He wiped away another tear, and then reached for her hand. Giving it a squeeze, he said, "Don't blame yourself, Catherine. You did nothing to cause this."

"Why, then?" More tears leaked from her eyes.

Stephen had uttered the same question just hours earlier, his emotional pain as acute as hers was now. As much as he wanted to hate her, he couldn't. And he didn't want to see her like this—devastated over the prospect of losing his cousin's child. Still, he had to know.

"Do you still love him?"

When she just looked at him blankly, he said, "Derek. Even after everything he did, do you still love him?"

"I don't love him, Stephen. After these past several months with you I realize I never loved him, not the way I should have. Love isn't a tepid emotion, and that's all I felt when I was with him."

Left unsaid was what they both knew: nothing that had transpired between them could be considered merely tepid.

"I'll take you back to your room."

"No, please." She clutched his hand. "Let me stay with you. I don't want to be alone right now."

"Catherine—"

"Just hold me, Stephen. Tomorrow will come soon enough. Just give me tonight. Let me pretend everything is going to be all right. That's all I'm asking of you. Please."

He was not cold-hearted enough to deny her request. And so he slipped into bed beside her, wrapped his arms around her slender body and let himself pretend as well.

CHAPTER ELEVEN

THEY didn't speak as they sat in the doctor's waiting room. Words seemed unnecessary, and what was there to say, really? Stephen had made his feelings well known to her the night before. He didn't love her. He didn't trust her.

The bleeding had stopped early that morning, and the cramping had subsided as well, but Catherine's nerves remained taut. Her world seemed to have been turned upside down in the past twenty-four hours, and she was still reeling.

A door opened and a pastel-coated nurse emerged.

"Catherine Danbury?" the nurse called out.

Catherine stood.

"Come on back to examination room one."

When Stephen remained seated, the nurse said, "Your husband can come, too."

"I'll wait here."

She wanted him with her, just as she had last night. But the sun had risen, and with the new day he'd apparently taken her at her word that she would ask nothing else of him.

The examination room was small and cold, especially since Catherine was dressed in nothing but an aqua paper gown that afforded her no warmth and little modesty. The nurse rolled a machine into the room, explaining that it would allow the doctor to perform an ultrasound to better determine the baby's status.

"We don't do this for everybody, since it can be quite costly. But with a last name like Danbury..." The nurse winked. "Well, we know you're not worried about whether or not your health insurer will cover it."

The test wasn't particularly comfortable, but she focused on the doctor, trying to read her diagnosis in his expression.

Finally, Catherine could stand the silence no longer. "Is my baby going to be okay?"

"I can't make any guarantees, Mrs. Danbury. But everything looks normal right now."

"What about the bleeding? The cramps?"

"It's not uncommon for women to experience spotting and cramping in their first trimester; sometimes it's nothing to worry about, and sometimes..." He shrugged. "Nature has a way of taking care of itself, and there is nothing medical science can do about it, I'm afraid. But try not to worry about that. As I said, things look fine."

"Is there anything I can do?"

He took off his glasses and stuffed them into the pocket of his white coat. "Take it easy. Stay off your feet for the next few days. Above all, try to relax. I'll see you in another month."

As the doctor left the nurse winked at Catherine.

"My advice, honey, is to make your husband wait on you for a change. I've got four kids, and let me tell you I milked every pregnancy for all it was worth. I even got a remodeled kitchen out of the last one."

Catherine tried to smile, but couldn't. Hormones, combined with worry and heartbreak, had tears blurring her vision.

"Come on, sweetie, there's no reason to cry," the nurse said, giving Catherine's hand a reassuring squeeze. "Just take a look at this."

She turned the screen so that Catherine could see, and pointed.

"There he—or she—is. Too soon to determine the sex, but you can make out the arms and legs."

"Oh, my." Wonder filled her. The image showed tiny arms and legs, completely out of proportion with the rest of the body, but the baby was beautiful, perfect, and the love she'd felt since she'd first learned about this new life swelled until she couldn't contain it any longer.

"Get my husband, please. I want him to see this."

Stephen didn't know what to expect when he walked into the examination room. It certainly wasn't Catherine, sitting on the edge of the table in a flimsy paper gown, crying and smiling at the same time.

"Look." She pointed at the screen. "Just look how perfect."

He studied the image and tried to be as enthusiastic as she was, but his heart was too heavy. Even so, he was happy for her.

"Everything's okay, then?"

"The doctor said to take it easy for a few days, but…yes, everything is okay."

"I'm glad. I don't wish you ill. I know how much this baby means to you."

Her smile dimmed, turned sad. "I know. I'll…I'll be making arrangements to move out today."

"It doesn't have to be done today. Wait until you're feeling better. There's no rush."

"Thank you, but I think we both need space right now."

She reached for his hand and threaded her fingers through his. Part of him never wanted to let her go.

"No matter what happens between us, Stephen, I will always love you."

He stumbled back a step, stared at her, sure he had not heard right.

"I love you," she repeated. "I had hoped, but… Well, it doesn't matter what I'd hoped. Still, it doesn't change what I feel, what I will always feel. And I wanted you to know."

He didn't respond. He couldn't. He returned to the waiting room and sank into one of the stiff-backed chairs, flummoxed. She loved him. Even though she was carrying his cousin's child, her heart belonged to Stephen. She had declared her feelings and he found he couldn't doubt her. Not when she was also determined to make arrangements to walk out of his life.

Looping a piece of tinsel from the Christmas tree that had been set up in the waiting room's corner around his finger, he recalled the past several months with Catherine. Even if she had already been pregnant when they married, he hadn't imagined the sparks that had ignited between them. Something was pressing at him now, a pressure building until it overwhelmed him, forcing him to see the truth once and for all. She loved him, and, despite her baby's paternity, he loved her in return. He had had the good fortune to stumble upon something rare, precious, and he had to do something quickly to keep from letting it slip away.

Tucking the strand of tinsel into his pocket, he came to a decision.

Their car was parked on the sixth floor of the adjacent parking structure. He waited until the elevator's other occupants exited before he hit the emergency stop button between floors five and six. The alarm sounded and Catherine gaped at him.

"What are you doing?"

"What I should have done weeks ago, when I first planned it." He bent down on one knee, pulled the strand of tinsel from his pocket. She offered no resistance when he took her left hand and tied the silver strand around her fourth finger.

"I have a real ring at home, I promise. It was my mother's. I had planned to give it to you a while ago, but then…" He shook his head. "I've been a fool, Catherine. A first-class fool. I don't deserve you, but I do love you."

He watched her lips quiver with what he hoped was the beginnings of a smile.

"I want you to be my wife. I want the vows we exchanged in Vegas to be for real. I promise to honor and cherish you. I promise to love you in sickness and in health, for richer and poorer. And I promise to love your baby as much as I love you."

"Oh, Stephen." She covered her mouth with one hand and began to cry in earnest.

"Don't cry, *querida*. I'll make a good father. Give me a chance." He squeezed her hand, kissed the back of it. "Please, please, give me a chance."

When she just continued to cry, he lowered his head. Too late, he thought. I am too late.

Catherine stared down at Stephen's bent head and then reached out to stroke his cheek. Hearing the words was sweeter than she could have imagined.

"It's a very good thing I love you so much," she said on a watery sigh.

"Why is that?"

"Because that's the only way I can forgive you for believing, even now, that this child is Derek's."

The elevator began to move, but Catherine doubted that was why her husband fell back until he was sitting on the floor.

"Mine? I'm...? We're...?"

"That's right. And now to answer your earlier question, yes, I want to stay married to you, too."

He was still holding her hand, so she used it to help pull him to his feet.

"Kiss me."

When the elevator doors swung open on the sixth floor a dozen people were waiting to board, but Catherine and Stephen were too busy renewing their vows to notice.

EPILOGUE

"ANOTHER deep breath," Stephen coached. "That's it, Catherine, you're doing great."

She watched him wince slightly as she gave his hand another vise-like squeeze. But he didn't pull away. He stayed where he was, fingers caught in her white-knuckled grip, something solid to hold on to as a fierce pain lanced her abdomen.

Her hold slackened as the contraction ebbed. His grew firmer.

He bent near and whispered in her ear. *"Te amo, querida."*

She found the energy to smile. "I love you, too."

"It will be over soon," the nurse promised. "You'll welcome you new baby into the world and all this pain will be forgotten."

Truer words…Catherine mused. She and Stephen had weathered enough turbulent seas even before she'd learned of her pregnancy. But soon all the confusion and doubt, as well as the past two months of doctor-ordered bedrest, would be worth it.

The pain began again, gathering like a storm cloud on the horizon before moving in with all the intensity of a hurricane breaking shore.

"It's time to push, Catherine," the doctor said.

Caught up as she was in the mission at hand, she heard Stephen's words of encouragement, felt him stroking the hair back from her damp forehead. She did the work, pushing and straining as her muscles protested and continued their merciless contraction. But there was no doubt in Catherine's mind that she and Stephen brought their child into the world together. They were a team, a unit. Made so not by the vows they'd exchanged in Las Vegas those many months ago, but by the love they shared, which grew stronger, grander and more encompassing each day.

"It's a girl," the doctor said, holding the squalling infant up for Catherine and Stephen to see.

"A girl," Stephen repeated, his voice a hoarse whisper. "We have a daughter."

A couple of hours later Catherine lay in bed in her hospital room, watching Stephen pace from the bassinet to the window. He'd been doing so for the past forty-five minutes.

"Have you decided on a name yet?" she asked. She'd left the choice up to him, although she'd long had something in mind.

He stopped, gently picked up their daughter. Cradling the baby in his arms, he said, "I'd like to name her Galena Rosaria, after my mother and aunt."

"It's a lovely name," Catherine replied, resisting the urge to smile smugly. Not long after she'd discovered she was pregnant she'd decided they should name their child after Stephen's mother if it was a girl or his father if it was a boy.

"Of course we can call her Gail," Stephen said.

"No."

"No?"

"I won't have all the poetry removed from her name. We will call her Galena. Galena Rosaria Danbury."

The names rolled from her tongue. Her accent had improved dramatically in the past several months, thanks to Stephen's grandmother and aunts. After Sunday dinners, as they washed dishes in the kitchen, they taught Catherine various words and phrases. She was far from fluent, but determined to get there. Determined that their daughter would someday be proud of her diverse heritage and conversant in her paternal relatives' native tongue.

Sitting on the edge of the bed, sleeping infant snug in the crook of his arm, Stephen gazed down at his wife.

"I never thought I'd say this, but I owe Derek a huge debt of gratitude. Thanks to his scheming, I have you."

She pulled him toward her for a kiss, and then said, "I'll save my gratitude for my mother."

"Your mother?"

"Well, she is the one who hired the wedding planner."

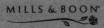

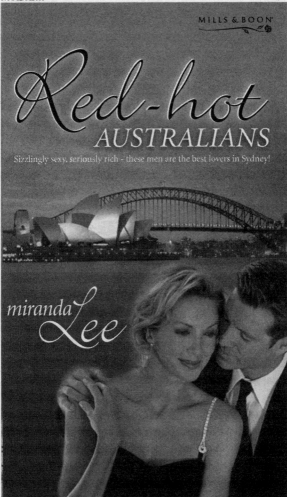

FREE
4 BOOKS
AND A SURPRISE GIFT!

We would like to take this opportunity to thank you for reading this Mills & Boon® book by offering you the chance to take FOUR more specially selected titles from the Tender Romance™ series absolutely FREE! We're also making this offer to introduce you to the benefits of the Reader Service™——

- ★ FREE home delivery
- ★ FREE monthly Newsletter
- ★ FREE gifts and competitions
- ★ Exclusive Reader Service discount
- ★ Books available before they're in the shops

Accepting these FREE books and gift places you under no obligation to buy; you may cancel at any time, even after receiving your free shipment. Simply complete your details below and return the entire page to the address below. *You don't even need a stamp!*

YES! Please send me 4 free Tender Romance books and a surprise gift. I understand that unless you hear from me, I will receive 6 superb new titles every month for just £2.69 each, postage and packing free. I am under no obligation to purchase any books and may cancel my subscription at any time. The free books and gift will be mine to keep in any case.

N4ZEF

Ms/Mrs/Miss/Mr ....Initials ....
BLOCK CAPITALS PLEASE

Surname ....

Address ....

....

....Postcode ....

Send this whole page to:
UK: FREEPOST CN81, Croydon, CR9 3WZ
EIRE: PO Box 4546, Kilcock, County Kildare (stamp required)

Offer valid in UK and Eire only and not available to current Reader Service subscribers to this series. We reserve the right to refuse an application and applicants must be aged 18 years or over. Only one application per household. Terms and prices subject to change without notice. Offer expires 30th September 2004. As a result of this application, you may receive offers from Harlequin Mills & Boon and other carefully selected companies. If you would prefer not to share in this opportunity please write to The Data Manager at PO Box 676, Richmond, TW9 1WU.

Mills & Boon® is a registered trademark owned by Harlequin Mills & Boon Limited.
Tender Romance™ is being used as a trademark.
The Reader Service™ is being used as a trademark.